Critical Acclaim for Penelope Gilliatt

"Perhaps because Miss Gilliatt has written two novels, these stories have the tense carrying power we all hope for in a book of short stories but more often find in a good novel. These are fresh, exact passionate reports on the permanent pains of youth, the elegiac self-knowledge of old age, fame, victory and defeat. Every story gives us not only the rare, old-fashioned pleasure of a well-told tale, but the exhilaration of having learned something new about the head and the heart" – *Lillian Hellman*

"Penelope Gilliatt is one of our really distinctive talents, a true original" – *Rebecca West*

"A wondrously undissembling compassion, a resplendent intelligence, and a boundlessly inventive wit . . . all the stories are brilliant but some are more amazingly so than others" – *Jean Stafford*

"For the devotee of the short story this is a collection which must be read: startlingly original, genuinely funny, and very, very touching" – *Illustrated London News*

"Miss Gilliatt writes beautifully – not only are her stories touching and filled with insight, but her style is refreshingly clear. She celebrates the bittersweet human condition in prose that brings us her visions undistorted. It is a pleasure to recommend this excellent collection, rich with awareness and intelligence" – *Los Angeles Times*

"Penelope Gilliatt's third book . . . is a superb accomplishment, and serves as a showcase for her fine intelligence, her rich, fresh, metaphorical prose style, and her uninhibited capacity for empathy and compassion" – *Saturday Review*

"Every story in *What's It Like Out?* comes off . . . Penelope Gilliatt is sad, funny and unobtrusively horrible, but never, never random" – *Punch*

"Known for her novels – *One By One* and *A State of Change* – and for her film criticism, Penelop Gilliatt now emerges, with this startling and marvellously funny book, as a master of the classical short story. Character and narrative have lately been losing ground in fiction, but not in the fiction of Miss Gilliatt. For her, character is crucial and narrative thrives. In a period in which observation is thought to have failed us, and we look inward, she looks out, and sees. And, with the written word itself having been called into question, she celebrates the word. In these nine stories there are no approximations, no evasions, no studied confusions. The air is crystalline. The characters are in plain view, and their voices carry. Miss Gilliatt comes to us with fresh and exact reports on corruption, melancholy, old age, eminence, great friendship, loneliness and defeat. Disclosing the vulnerability of the favoured as well as the unfavoured, she records particulars of behaviour and gradations of feeling that ordinarily go unperceived. She does not turn away from the dark disorder of existence but defiantly brings to bear on it a powerful intelligence, a benevolent wit, passion, style and pure sanity. She leaves us exhilarated."

William Shawn, 1968

PENELOPE GILLIATT

was born in London in 1932 and brought up in Northumberland where she was privately tutored. She attended Queen's College, London and Bennington College, Vermont. She also studied music theory, harmony and counterpoint and trained in the piano, harpsichord and clavichord.

Penelope Gilliatt has contributed regularly to newspapers and magazines. From 1961 to 1967 she was the film critic of the *Observer* and, for one year, exchanged roles with Kenneth Tynan, becoming theatre critic. In 1967 she became the film critic for *The New Yorker*, for which she continues to write, contributing profiles and short stories as a contracted writer.

Her first collection of short stories, *What's It Like Out?*, appeared in 1968 and was followed by *Nobody's Business* (1972); *Splendid Lives* (1978); *Quotations from Other Lives* (1982), *They Sleep Without Dreaming* (1985) and *22 stories* (1986). Her five novels are: *One By One* (1965); *A State of Change* (1967); *The Cutting Edge* (1979); *Moral Matters* (1983) and, most recently, *A Woman of Singular Occupation* (1988). Penelope Gilliatt was also the author of the multi-award winning screenplay, *Sunday Bloody Sunday* (1971), which was nominated for an Oscar. Her other dramatic work includes a double bill of one-act plays, a three-act libretto for the English National Opera and plays and films for television (including *Living on the Box*, adapted from the story of the same name in this collection).

Penelope Gilliatt is a Fellow of the Royal Society of Literature and has received a grant in recognition for her creative work from the American Academy of Arts and Letters. She is currently engaged in a new work of non-fiction to be published on both sides of the Atlantic. She has travelled widely, especially in France, Italy, India, America, Poland, Czechoslovakia and Turkey and has one daughter, Nolan.

VIRAGO
MODERN
CLASSIC

NUMBER

317

PENELOPE GILLIATT

WHAT'S IT LIKE OUT?

AND OTHER STORIES

Published by VIRAGO PRESS Limited 1989
20-23 Mandela Street, Camden Town, London NW1 0HQ

This Anthology Copyright © Penelope Gilliatt

First published in Great Britain by Martin Secker & Warburg Limited 1968
Copyright © Penelope Gilliatt 1965, 1966, 1967, 1968

Acknowledgements
"The Redhead" originally appeared in *Transatlantic Review*; the other stories in
this collection were first published in *The New Yorker*. The author and
publishers are grateful to the editors for permission to reprint these stories.

British Librarty Cataloguing in Publication Data

Gilliatt, Penelope
  What's It Like Out?
  I. Title
  823′.913 [F]
  ISBN: 1-85381-016-9

Printed in Finland by Werner Söderström Oy

Contents

Fred and Arthur

"Friends, Romans, countrymen," shouted Fred Stokes at the top of the Forum steps, carrying Arthur Moe in his arms centre stage. They wore togas, sandals, and short white socks. Fred was thin, Arthur very fat, and Fred's head made a pecking movement over the bulk of his friend with the effort of bearing the load.

Arthur felt anxiety in the grip and spoke into the the pullet neck on the upstage side. "You've got your weight wrong."

"Lend me your ears," Fred orated, altering his hold and guttering at the knees.

"It's your right foot."

"I come to bury Caesar, not to praise him" Fred was still concentrated on his clasp instead of his balance, and getting sworn at for it. Their manager, standing in the wings, wondered what Arthur was yakking about, and at the same time had a moment of seeing them as Gandhi carrying a buffalo.

"I'll have to do a fall," Arthur muttered. He gathered his great weight neatly to a point against Fred's sickly-looking chest, said "Serve you right" in a cheery tone under the roar of the music-hall audience and shoved away, grounding delicately at the foot of the Forum steps and watching his partner with one eye. Fred was thundering on with the speech as though the corpse hadn't fled, and at the same time bobbing up onto the balls of his feet with relief from the lost burden. Arthur scrutinized the business and thought it makeshift but not bad. He started taking apart the engineering of the scene, keeping count of the timing in his head.

They went back to their dressing-room in a hurry as soon as the act was over, and Arthur started a metronome. Fred tucked his toga between his legs like a baby's nappy and picked his friend up.

"I don't see what I did different," he said, facing front to inspect the two of them in the mirror and then turning round to have a look from the side.

"I told you. Your weight was on the wrong foot. It still is. You can't hardly manœuvre."

"It wasn't bad, what we did."

"Best get it straight the old way first. Seventeen, eighteen, *Lend me your ears*, then my sneeze on nineteen, and your slap on twenty."

"I like the fall better myself," Fred said. "Let's keep it. Long time since we did a fall."

"Bit old-fashioned, isn't it?" said Arthur.

"What are you talking about? Falls don't date."

"Take it from fourteen," said Arthur.

"*Friends, Romans.* My shoulders is busting."

"Fifteen, sixteen. Carry on, I'm counting. You've got to *come to*. Nineteen, twenty."

"*Bury Caesar, not to.* Now I'm on my left foot. Suppose I stay on it. *Praise him.*"

"Twenty-four, twenty-five."

"Are you going or not? I said *praise him*. That's where

you did it before." Fred watched carefully in the mirror for some muscular indication of what his friend had in mind.

The bulk lay poleaxed. "Twenty-five," it said again.

"*The evil that men do.* You've gone and left it far too late. *Lives after them, the good is oft interrèd with their bones.* You'll have to go, I've run out of words." But by now Arthur had quit, flying smoothly through the air like a zeppelin and saying "Thirty-one, thirty-two" as he went. "All right," he said, rolling lightly onto the floor. "Again."

Their manager came into the room. "If you don't keep in that fall, I'm stopping your sweets," he said, and then looked down at the mass of Arthur on the ground. "I haven't seen you do one like that since your old dad was alive."

"It's all in the position of the head," said Fred, sitting down and having a beer. "I can't do it. Not like he can. You use the head as the rudder." He stopped the metronome and put his hands on his bony kneecaps, looking into the mirror at his gloomy Indian-brave's face.

Arthur watched him, pulled in his stomach, listened to the loudspeaker to hear how the performing dog was doing, and thought seriously enough that he hadn't seen Fred so exhilarated since last August at Blackpool. "Good date, this. I've always liked Huddersfield," he said.

"You're putting on weight," said the manager, picking up Arthur's belt and looking at the notches.

"No, he's not," Fred said loyally. "That's muscle."

After the second house the two of them went out to supper. It was their ninth year together, and they had been top of the bill at the Palladium in the West End six years running. It was a buoyant evening. They had four pints of

beer each and a slap-up dinner in one of Huddersfield's
new swinging joints.

"Changed a bit," said Arthur, looking at a girl dancing
in a mini-skirt not much deeper than a belt.

"My old dad used to sing Handel here in the working-
men's choir," Fred said. "Came up from London by coach.
They like Handel here. Here and Newcastle."

"Newcastle's a good date, too."

Arthur and Fred had been to school together. Their
partnership seemed freakishly fortunate. When they went
out on their own with girls, they tended to fix things for the
same evening so as not to spend two nights separated where
one would do. Fred's father had owned a pub near a music
hall where Arthur's father had often played, and before
their sons were even born the men had sometimes had
Saturday-night booze-ups together. Arthur's father had
been a famous comic called Willie Moe, and his mother,
Queenie, was the butt in Willie's routine. When he married
her, she was a reserved, very plain girl who played the harp
in a provincial symphony orchestra. She had learned the
harp because she had once been told that she had beautiful
elbows, and harp playing seemed to make better use than
most careers of the Lord's stingy gift. Her husband admired
her serious-mindedness, and at the same time saw that her
absence of humour held comic promise for his act. He
would plant her downstage and get her to start playing "I
dreamt that I dwelt in marble halls," and then sabotage her
work from the back wall.

As soon as the infant Arthur was old enough to be
propped against the proscenium arch, he was included in
the turn. There was nothing else to do with him; theatrical

landladies didn't offer babysitting with the rent. When he strayed, his mother would shove him back into position with her foot as she harped. Then one night the child fell onto the bass drum, plummeting ten feet into the orchestra pit without seeming to harbour a grudge, and it occurred to his father to try bouncing him. Arthur commanded fame and respect in the profession for several years as "The Living Football", followed by "The Living Boomerang" and "The Living Dart". The characterizations consisted of being rolled up into a sphere by Willie, or swung by one arm, or aimed at a dartboard while wearing a trick suction device on his head. The cap fixed him securely to the board, with his airborne body trembling behind him like the handle of a plunged dagger. Later on, when he was five and too heavy to play a dart satisfactorily, he became "The Living Gladstone Bag". He wore a handle on the back of his costume, stitched there by his hard-driven mother herself because she wasn't going to have some theatrical costumier treating her son as if he were a sequin. His on-stage father would unsnap the child's clothes, which were held together at the back by a clasp, pack them with toothbrush, pyjamas, and reading matter, and throw the patient luggage at an assistant stage manager dressed as a railway porter. The boy went without a name until he was six. His father dismissed the notion that it was any necessity and called for his son by clearing his throat, like Henry Irving demanded a prompt. His mother felt wretched about the matter and often suggested Roland. She liked this name because it was romantic and well-bred, which were precisely Willie Moe's objections to it. Her alternative was Percy; Willie said it was wet, and she said it was "Henry

IV". When she moaned and said, well, what did he suggest instead, Willie would affably juggle the child and two oranges, and reply with the obvious oath. And his wife would flinch at the coarse life that harp-playing had brought her to, and go off her kipper, and mash up the remains with some potatoes for the boy's breakfast next morning. If her son hadn't got a name, at least she was going to see that he had a proper lining to his stomach. He went to bed on porridge, got up on potatoes, and did his twice-nightly work on scones, baps, cottage loaves, crumpets, and Yorkshire parkin. The boy adored his father exclusively; his mother's recourse was starch, and his bulk therefore waxed and waxed. The process didn't perturb him for the simple reason that it didn't repel Willie. The jibes of the kids at his scattered schools, which he attended sometimes for a token day or two to throw a sop to the government, struck him as neither here nor there. What he watched for anxiously was any sign that his father found fatness unprofessional. But on the contrary Willie made it seem a prop of the work, like ripe thighs in a chorus girl or the swivel eye of Ben Turpin. Nor was it a disadvantage technically. The child was agile enough to seem filled with helium, as if he had mass without weight.

He was named on his seventh birthday. His mother had hopelessly suggested Cyril. Willie Moe snorted and picked up the boy by the leg and started to whirl him as if winding him up, which was part of a new routine called "The Living Propeller". Then he dropped the weight with a glow on his face and said, "I've got it."

"What?" his wife asked.

"Arthur," he said, pronouncing it "Arfer" because he

was a Cockney of the old generation. "Arfer Moe. 'Alf a mo. We can work it into the act."

His wife felt unspeakably lowered and lit the gas for the baked beans. Everything was grist.

The child's own feelings were split between mortification at a christening that doomed him to live out for good a pun that he could already see to be gruesome and pride that his father had cared for him enough to embed him into his act by the very roots of his name. The ambiguity lasted long after Willie died. So did Arthur's torn attitude to his weight. He could never entirely regret it, because it reminded him of working with Willie, and the passing resolves he made as a grown-up to lose some of it always contained a tang of un-ease about betraying his professional qualifications in the eyes of a man who would have belted him for such a thing.

After Willie's death Queenie packed in the theatre. She gave harp lessons and sent her son firmly to school. It was wartime and the boys called him Barrage Balloon. The normal childhood that other people wished on him struck him as mostly plaguing and tawdry; his own lost norm, a life spent in the company of ribald sopranos and tap-dancers and hard-pressed comedians in fear of the sack, seemed to have more decency and purpose. When Fred Stokes arrived at the school, Arthur had spent a year in hell. But as soon as their friendship was struck the memory faded and the bad time seemed no worse than some null interlude between two boon companions. To be with Fred was as naturally convivial as to be with Willie. At the age of nine Fred was already very much like the man he was going to be at thirty-five or forty. He was tacit, bold, and weedy, with a miraculous sense of humour at work behind the face of a tomahawk. He could make his friend laugh convulsively enough to fall off schoolroom chairs, and once even out of a hammock. Arthur would lie on the floor heaving, dead silent apart from a rust creak at the moments when he managed to catch a breath. Within himself he would have a sensation of liquefying with giggles and of becoming extremely thin, like a puddle.

The two fitted together even in the way the day took them. Fred woke up lugubriously, and the spectacle of Arthur's capacious morning optimism lifted his spirits. After the last show, or earlier if they weren't working, Arthur would often fall prey to the bite of melancholy, with such sharp dread of all endings that he would greatly fear going to sleep, as if nothing would be left to him unless he kept watch on it. He hated other people's leaving him for bed, and when he saw a hard mood ahead he often took a sleeping pill at supper to stop himself from being clamorous, though at the same time he found his terror about the end of a day daft in a creature who was surely intended by build to signify immortal fun.

While they were walking back from the Huddersfield discothèque, it suddenly dawned on Fred and Arthur that they had eaten three main meals that day instead of two. The usual sausages and spuds had been brought to them between the shows.

"We had lunch. That's what put us out," Arthur said. A producer had fed them silly in an effort to woo them to do a film. Arthur had eaten large helpings of scampi and steak-and-kidney pudding, refrained from the damson pie as a gesture, and taken his mind off the others' plates by saying that they would do the film if he and Fred were allowed to write it, direct it, find the props, and put together the sound track. He also said that he would want to do his own stunt work in an escape sequence. The appalled producer took refuge in the unions and his insurance company, and Fred and Arthur composed their faces into the necessary combination of artistic bloody-mindedness and guestly sympathy to scotch the project without actually seeming to throw their good lunch back into the producer's face. Neither of them had liked him at all.

"I've never had a good experience of a boss with a short upper lip," said Fred.

"The scampi was OK," Arthur said, bumping a penny along the railings in groups of four and muttering "Breakfast, lunch, dinner, supper ... Breakfast, lunch, dinner, supper. No more than the Tudors had, I bet."

"You should have had the damson pie," Fred said.

"No, I shouldn't. I'm blowing up again."

Nearer to their hotel, Fred did an improvisation about the home life of an air hostess who was taken over in bed by her working phrases and asked her husband if he would care to recline and have a beverage. Arthur leaned against a lamp-post and felt thinned.

The mirror in their tatty hotel suite exposed that delusion. "My face looks as if it's going to drop off a fruit tree," he said at himself. "It's like a medlar. *Purple*. It seems to be *running*."

"It's the light," Fred said.

The telephone rang. Arthur left Fred to it and lay on his back in his own bedroom, reading a book about ballistics. He felt himself to be so uneducated that it seemed hopeless even to try to catch up with the ordinary things that people knew.

"Daisy said to give you her love," Fred said, coming into the room half an hour later. Daisy was Fred's bird, a freckled teenager with red tabby hair whom Arthur had entrusted with a slice of his savings so that she could open a boutique. He often caught himself liking her better than his own girl-friend. Perhaps this was because she belonged to Fred, which meant that there was no call to—Oh, all that, he thought, shutting up in his own head. He had a striking decorum even in his thoughts. Fred sat on the end of the bed with his elbows on his knees and his hands hanging down with their knuckles back to back, like a tired football player in a dressing-room. He was looking at a beautiful textbook about racehorses that Arthur had laid out on the floor.

"She says the shop's raking it in," he said. "She's going to pay you back the loan at the end of the week."

"No hurry."

"You like making people's fortunes for them, don't you?" Fred said.

Arthur immediately started to tell a story about a time in music hall when he had set out to behave less admirably and had cost a theatre manager a packet. After a couple of sentences he went into the present tense, which was a habit he had in speaking of the past, as if it were the plot of some play he was about to do. "So even the performing seals are disgusted with his cheeseparing by now, and that night the lyric soprano breaks one of the hoops of her crinoline in the middle of her best love song because he wouldn't run to proper whalebone, and I take myself aside and say to myself...." This was another characteristic that he had: he often talked about himself as if he had custody of someone who needed a lot of upbringing.

"Tell that story to Daisy sometime," Fred said at the end of it.

"You two should get married," said Arthur, scaring himself. His thoughts teetered nastily, and he wondered if he had uttered the possibility in order to ward it off.

"Why don't you marry Peg?" Fred rinsed the old tea out of a cup and poured some Scotch and tap water into it.

"It mightn't suit the work."

"What?"

"We'd be three, and all that." But the same thing was true of Fred's marrying Daisy. "It would be different if it was you and Daisy. I mean, I like her."

"I like Peg."

"Anyway, I'm too fat to get married."

"Don't be so sorry for yourself."

"I'm not sorry. I'm just fat."

"What about King Farouk? He never stopped getting married."

They hadn't spoken like this before. Arthur tightened. Constraint stung his skin like a wave of hornets. The conversation was alien and impossible. At the same time he had the clearest image in his mind of the three of them: Fred, Daisy, and himself, and it was a spectacle of nothing but pleasure. He was hanging his head over the edge of the bed and wondering what to do next when a spring burst in the mattress.

"I still think you should try marrying Peg," Fred said, starting for the door and giving Arthur as sharp a seizure as he had ever had of longing and hatred for an ally who was deserting him to go to sleep. "You could always split up," said his friend. Another ending. A second swarm of enemies attacked Arthur's skin and he swore at them blue murder.

"I've got a new idea for the fall," he said. "I keep the arms still and move off from your downstage shoulder. Your weight's on your back foot, same as before, but now you can brace it better against the step." Peg was all right, but to marry her seemed a deal of foreign new trouble to face for the sake of off-loading the known old pain of loneliness before sleep. He remembered some story about a primitive farmer who discovered roast pork when his house and his pig barn burned down and then imagined that he had to set fire to the place again every time he fancied a bit of crackling. "Hang on to the house," said Arthur, taking himself aside. "Hang on to the house." He lay on his elbow and hip along the top of a bureau, looking more like a Turkish sultan in a harem than he felt. Then he flung himself neatly across to the bed, thinking agreeably of life with Fred and Daisy as he went, and another spring broke. Mankind (me), he thought, mashing up the rest of the mattress because he wasn't going to spend the night braced for a lot of bedsprings to bust in their own time, is idyllic in his intentions, tragic in his fate, and farcical in his functions.

No: *ludicrous*, he thought next morning, when the first thing in his waking head was the image of his sealion self with a wife.

Fred and Daisy got married later that year. Arthur was their best man and there were jolly pictures of the wedding in the papers. He took them out on a spree the night before, just the three of them.

"It's a stag night, only with a girl," he said. "You don't want a lot of people, do you?"

Daisy asked Fred privately whether they shouldn't get him to invite Peg. Fred had already thought of it and shook his head.

At the Savoy Grill, Arthur told Daisy that they were going to drink Dom Pérignon. "We've gone off beer since you decided to get spliced," he said, looking at Fred.

"*Fred* hasn't. *We* always drink beer," said Daisy, collaring the "we". Then she regretted it, and touched Arthur's arm and laughed. "I don't know anything about wine. Is Dom Pérignon good?"

"Also very pricey," said Fred.

"That's what money's for," Arthur said.

Fred said, "The only other time he ever ordered it was the night you rang us up in Leeds to say you'd got the house and we could move in by the week we were spliced."

Then Arthur took them to a night club called The Scotch, and made them dance, and thought they looked good together. "Half the room is wearing clothes they've brought from your posh shop," he said to Daisy. "Best investment I ever made was in that place. In fact, the *only* one I ever made."

"Haven't you got any stocks and shares, then?"

"He hardly even trusts the bank," Fred said. "I know what he means. He'd much sooner keep it in an old pair of tights."

"What you put into the business," Daisy said, "you should have treated it as a loan and let me pay you back the capital. I always thought of it as a loan. Two thousand quid is a lot of loot. You might need it. Or I might go bankrupt."

"I like getting dividends," said Arthur. "The other day I got twenty-two pounds five and six from your accountants. It seems like real money, your dividends. Like getting a wage packet again, instead of voting myself a salary as my own director or whatever it is they make me do."

He saw them off on honeymoon and didn't know what to do with the weeks they were going to be away, until he thought of taking a total-immersion course in Italian. Daisy had once said that the three of them might spend a holiday together next year in San Gimignano. He worked at the course twelve hours a day and found it exhausting but staggeringly easy. Once he was over the edge of extreme fatigue his brain drank up the language by the pint. He thought of startling Fred and Daisy with a flood of Italian when he met them off the boat train at Victoria Station, but at the sight of them his plans fled for excitement. Intruding on a newly married couple sounded a textbook mistake when he surveyed it, but plainly both of them were glad he was there; he could see it in their faces and ran up the platform with joy, not shy at all about the reflection of his hurtling bulk in the glass of a newsagent's stall.

It was a couple of months before he felt in Daisy's way. He tried to find himself a new girl to take his mind off it: some new girl, because Peg had gone wrong. He invented engagements when he had nothing to do, and ordered *La Stampa* to keep up his Italian as a surprise for Fred when the present stage was over. Surely it was too predictable that Daisy was going to want to elbow him out; the feelings that existed between the three of them were substantial enough to forbid anything so trite. He started keeping Fred and himself to timetables, so that she knew where she was, and cut out eating with Fred after the show or seeing him in the daytime at weekends. Working together was more enviable than ever, and professionally they seemed infallible. By good luck, they were in the middle of a long stint in London. The next provincial tour was months ahead, and by then Fred would have seen Daisy through whatever was bothering her. Arthur liked her very much, and when he heard from Fred that she was going into hospital overnight to have a minor operation he packed her room with flowers and clownish notes. Fred was jumpy while they were working together the next morning, so Arthur opened a bottle of Bollinger in their businesslike new office and then took him out to lunch.

"What's she in there for?" he said.

"Children," said Fred.

Arthur changed the champagne to Dom Pérignon. They had two bottles. He looked at his watch. "Is it over yet?"

"I don't know."

"When were they doing it, then?"

"I don't know."

"You don't *know*?"

"She didn't want me to think about it too much. She just went in last night and said she'd be back today as soon as she could. She wouldn't let me take her."

"I understand that," Arthur said. "She knew you'd hate the lousy place. Couldn't she have had it done at home?"

"She doesn't mind hospitals like you do."

They had a brandy, and then another. Arthur saw Fred looking at his watch. "Do you want to go?" he said.

"I don't much want to be at home on my own. She won't be back for ages."

"Let's have a Calvados."

They forgot the hospital and invented a new sketch. The restaurant closed in the end, so Arthur took Fred to Fortnum's and they floated through the food department arm in arm. They ordered chicken breasts in jelly and invalid grapes for Daisy, and grouse in aspic to be sent when she was better. Then they went down the stairs to the wine counter and Arthur bought Fred some port—a lot of port, what the noble-nosed assistant called a *pipe* of port. Arthur told the lordly one that it was to be sent to Mr and Mrs Stokes, but Fred knew whom it was tacitly meant for, because he had read in newspaper gossip columns about dukes laying down pipes of port when heirs were born.

"Why do you hate hospitals so much?" Fred said when they had dropped into Jacksons of Piccadilly to buy Daisy some out-of-season strawberries that they hadn't thought of in Fortnum's.

"Dunno," Arthur said.

Fred waited and looked at him, knowing that only forbearance might call it out.

"Heart," Arthur said loudly. The morning-coated manager had recognized them and was being proprietary with them in front of a dowager customer. Taking the word— "heart" or "art"?—for a signal of entertainment, he brought his dowager nearer.

Fred, drunk though he was, saw what was happening and pushed Arthur toward the Stiltons. "The old bag's got her ear trumpet out," he said too clearly. "What do you mean, heart? All right, aren't you?"

"You know how it is," Arthur said.

Fred stumbled and steadied himself by putting his hand on a York ham. "Yes," he said. The dowager looked on and smiled and thought courteously about the people. Fred was suddenly felled with booze. "You're all right, though?" he said at last, holding on to a Gorgonzola.

"I always think the old thing's conking out, you see. They keep telling me it isn't, but it's all bluff, isn't it? Doctors. Look at the common cold. They don't even know about that. I mean, obviously I've got it coming. A man of my weight." He focused on a birthday cake that interested him. "I once saw a film about a girl in love with a man who had a dickey heart," he said. "I think he was a composer. Thin, of course."

"Anton Walbrook."

"Can't remember who the girl was. I wish it had been Carole Lombard . . . I'd like to have married Carole Lombard. Do you remember what we were doing when she was killed?"

"Bleeding French dictation."

"No we wasn't, it was bleeding basketwork. They was making us make *baskets*, for the *war effort*. Carole Lombard was a nice girl. She had the nicest forehead I ever saw." Arthur thought of her dead, and reacted to a reflection of his own mortal hulk with more sympathy toward it than usual. "Poor child."

"What do you mean, child? She wasn't any younger when she died than we are now."

"But she feels younger, because we've gone on living

longer," said Arthur. He glimpsed a fallacy, said "Longer to *us*, I mean" with a vague interest in nailing it, and then thought the hell with it and bought some very expensive soap. So after that they staggered happily to Hamley's in search of mechanical toys for themselves, and passed a record shop on the way that reminded Arthur of something. "Daft of me not to be able to remember who the girl was," he said, "but I tell you what I do remember. They played the Grieg Concerto every time the composer was going to have an attack."

He hummed and sounded quite at ease, so Fred asked if he would like the record.

"Thanks very much," Arthur said furiously. "I can never hear the damned thing without wanting a cardiogram."

When they got back to Fred's house, it was eight o'clock. They had had tea at the Ritz and drinks at the Café Royal, and then more drinks at Lyons' Corner House in Coventry Street because they were fed up with swish places and Lyons' seemed more like home. They were more than fairly high, merry as grigs, and prepared to go on all night.

Daisy had been back for a long time; she looked white and pinched. "Where have you been?" she said, crying. "I rang everyone. I was out of my mind with worry."

"Shopping," said Fred.

"He didn't think you'd be back for ages," Arthur said protectively.

"You're drunk," she said to Fred, and turned on Arthur. "You've made Fred drunk. How *could* you? When I was in *hospital*." She cried some more. "I came out faster than anyone's ever left before. As soon as I could walk straight, I got out. They said I had to lie down for two hours because

I was going to be groggy, but I thought Fred would be worried. I had to get back."

"You shouldn't have done that," Fred said.

"He's only drunk because he *was* worried," Arthur said.

"People should do what doctors say." Fred's voice was acid. "After operations."

"It wasn't an operation. How can you call it an *operation*? It was for a *baby*."

"You're being a soppy date," Arthur said. "Funny, you're not usually."

"Perhaps it's the anæsthetic," Fred said.

"Anæsthetics can upset people for hours," Arthur said.

Daisy screamed at them. "Stop ganging up. Even when I've been in *hospital*, for *this*, the two of you gang up."

The humiliation and jealousy that had surfaced in her didn't abate in the weeks ahead, and the prospect of the friends' provincial tour together made her behave like a vixen. She broke up the partnership with exhaustive cunning, prising Arthur away with weapons of sexual mortification that she knew he would never describe to a living soul, least of all to Fred, because she was Fred's loved wife. She made Fred see himself only as she described him—as a man who was deliberately making his now pregnant wife unhappy. All the same, he insisted on doing a final tour. He did it because he wanted to, because he wasn't going to be her victim, and because he cared very much for Arthur. The time together wasn't at all the funeral wake it might have been. On the contrary, it was brilliant and buoyant: two months of boon nights. They had actors' temperaments, and they forgot London because it wasn't there. Future

separation didn't exist, except when the long arm of the
telephone reached into the room.

"It's only for a time," Fred said on the last night of the
tour. "We'll give it till the baby's a year old, say. Or six
months. Probably she'll be so wrapped up in it she'll feel
differently."

Daisy had one baby and then another, and Fred and
Arthur did a television series together directly after the first
child was born, but a reserve had come between them and
their companionship wasn't quite the same. Arthur went
back to life alone in his rooms in South Kensington and
wondered how to proceed. He dipped into books, but
couldn't get his brain to bite. He went to Italy on his own
and eventually made himself pick up a girl in Rome, mostly
for the sake of having someone to speak his new Italian to,
but she thought his intense shyness some sort of perversion
and kicked him out. Arthur wandered the streets and ate
pasta on his own and learned the intricate history of Christian heresy in an Italian-language library. It was plainly not
a useful thing for a comedian to do. But then being a
comedian was plainly not a useful thing to do either. He
came back to England and went on drinking champagne
alone, and nerved himself to do a TV series without Fred.
The endeavour was professionally abysmal as well as painful, and his money started to run out. Life seemed more ex-
acting than God himself.

Then the Aldwych Theatre suddenly asked him to play
Bottom in *A Midsummer Night's Dream* for the Royal
Shakespeare Company. He waited until it was nearly too
late, and then set his alarm for the old confident time of the

morning and rang up his agent to tell him to say yes. As soon as the offer was accepted, it seemed the clearest piece of luck. Arthur remade his day, for he had let it disintegrate stupidly. His new habit of sleeping on and on to rid himself of as much time as possible and then of staying up drinking alone until very late only left him with none of his natural good time and hour upon hour of his bad. So he started getting up early again, at five or even four, and going into heavy sleep with the waning light. The work ahead began to make him feel over-rested and dangerous, like a fat lion. Every now and then he would walk through Covent Garden fruit market towards the Aldwych to make sure that the theatre was still there. He refrained from ringing Fred up and stored Daisy's dividend cheques in a drawer without cashing them, although he could have done with the money.

The rehearsals were as pleasurable as they generally are. The director was a small, pink-cheeked man with bottle-shaped shoulders and an expression of misleading blankness. He took rehearsals in an ancient overcoat that might have come from Gogol's dustbin. It hung to his mid-calves and he was devoted to it. Instead of talking from the stalls to actors in front of one another, he would always shamble up onto the stage with his peculiar hedgehog gait and take them aside separately. He spoke very shrewdly and at alarming speed, in a low voice that seemed to come from elsewhere; though his lips might be moving in front of Arthur, the shafts of help would sound as if they came from the wings or the orchestra pit. The director had a knack of giving elegant voice to exactly the thought that was currently in poorish shape at the back of Arthur's head, and this was infuriating, though to feel resentment at having your skull so stylishly looted seemed small-minded and a blunder of taste. Halfway through the rehearsals Arthur started to feel anxious, and after nights of floundering he concluded that he should stop trying to put aside what he knew from music hall. Next day, of course, the director shuffled up onto the stage, stopped the rehearsal, took Arthur on one side, and lifted the ass's mask to murmur, fluttering the hairs on the bearded jawbone, "You're cutting yourself off from your technique."

"I know," Arthur said impatiently. "I thought that Shakespeare . . . I mean, I thought—"

"Bottom is a music-hall character," said the director over him. "People always make him too pathetic. Try playing him as George Robey."

"Blast," Arthur said to himself. "There goes what I was thinking again."

After a traditionally disastrous dress rehearsal the director came into Arthur's dressing-room, which he shared with Flute the Bellows Mender, and said cheerily, "I tell you what, why don't you go back to the awful way you used to do it? Then the production will be integrated because it will be *all* bad."

"I think it's disgusting, him talking like that," Flute said afterwards in a thin voice. "As if the conception hadn't got anything to do with him." He slammed down a tin of cleansing cream. Flute was a mirthless man who often used words like "conception", "subtext", and "seminal", and also "Jarry-esque", which appeared to have something to do with a play called *Ubu Roi*. Four weeks of being cooped up with Flute had taught Arthur that *Ubu Roi* was the most seminal possible thing about funniness, and if it was a book he was prepared to try getting it out of the public library one day.

Arthur looked at Flute's cross face and thought longingly of Fred's horse sense at dress rehearsals. With as much robustness as he could spare, he said that he didn't think the director had meant to be flippant. This added fuel to Flute's chilly little fire, and Arthur's shoulder was given a painful thwack with a rolled-up copy of the *Tulane Drama Review*.

"Comedy should be taken seriously," Flute said.

Arthur grunted a serviceable yes or no, perfected in combat with supercilious wine waiters who had tried to test his strength, or his French, or both.

Cheek, he thought later, with his usual time lag, pouring himself a glass of champagne from the half-bottles that he kept in the fridge. He nearly rang Fred up, but he would be seeing him tomorrow at the first night. Then the telephone rang, and the director said he had been very good, and did he like pâté? Because his wife had made dishes of it as first-night presents for the cast, apart from Titania, who was on a diet and would have to be dealt with in some other way. At the idea of pâté in the offing, Arthur's voice leaped like a salmon. "Oh, blow Titania," he said, putting four fingers into his waistband, which was on the loose side at the moment. "Give her the pâté anyway and let her get on with it. She can always hand it on to Peaseblossom or Mustardseed. They both look starving."

"That's their ballet background," said the director.

"You could give yourself a nasty cut on those shoulder blades," Arthur said, suddenly remembering the whole girl subject after his respite from it and feeling unusually breezy.

The sight of Fred and Daisy after the first night added to his nerve, and he scooped the skeletal Peaseblossom out of a dressing-room full of tulle to take her out to dinner with them. She stayed mute through two rounds of drinks and potted shrimps.

"You *did* have a crush of fans in your dressing-room," said Daisy, doing her best.

"Mashed up Mustardseed's wings," Peaseblossom said.

"What?" Daisy asked.

Arthur inquired further and relayed his findings. Her colleague's fairy costume had been badly injured by an admirer who had sat on it.

"What rotten luck," Daisy said, putting on the upper-class voice that she used only when she was feeling guarded. But what about? Not about the sight of me *acting*, thought Arthur; surely not. He asked after Fred's new play and she ran on with unconvincing enthusiasm about a young actress who was going to be in it.

"She's a dish," said Fred. "Only sixteen. We'll all be up for child rape. I don't know whether she can act, but she looks a treat."

"She's the bird with the two Afghans," said Arthur, who had seen pictures of the dogs in the papers.

"She's a fearfully nice girl. Have you met her?" Daisy said graciously to Peaseblossom, who was in contemplation with spaghetti.

"You sound like a royal going round a factory," Fred said. He ladled some of his stew onto Daisy's plate. "Go on, shut your cake-hole with that." They laughed together with such intimacy that Arthur had to look away. Then Fred took Peaseblossom off to dance and Arthur gave

Daisy an envelope of the uncashed dividend cheques, saying that he wanted her to plough them back into the business. She missed the quality of his action altogether, or chose to pretend to, and said crisply, "Oh, you can tear them up, love. I had them stopped ages ago."

When Fred came back to the table, the two old friends suddenly fused and started to laugh, while Daisy had to wait upon them as their natural audience. "This is the way things really are, isn't it?" Arthur cried in his head. "It can't have been lost. Dear God, they'll pick their things up in a minute and leave me on my tod with that Peaseblossom. I'm tired, it's not fair. What shall I do with her when she's had enough to eat?" He took her back to her flat in Putney, which was a long way, and she turned out to be keen on cocoa. Arthur left her to a mug of it and a Beatles record.

He began to be asked to act in play after play. There was something awry with directors' reasons for casting him and something un-nourishing in the West End audiences' response, but he smothered the knowledge of it. Intellectual reviewers took him up in left-wing papers because of his music-hall background and appreciated him in a way that made him wretched. They wrote as though finding him funny were something radical and upright, of a kind with rallying goodwill toward coloured immigrants. One director used him in *Waiting for Godot,* and he felt at home in a straight play at last, but unfortunately a critic wrote four hundred words about the Christly nature of the moment when he took his hat off. After Arthur read that paralysing codswallop, the piece of business became impossible and it was only after Fred rang him up and ribbed him about it that he could manage to get the thing off his head again.

It was summer, though, and life was working in its careless way. Arthur went to the Kings Road one hot afternoon to buy some sausages at Sainsbury's.

"That's Arthur Moe," said a young man on the street outside. He looked like a male model.

"So it is," said his girl friend.

"Ask him for his autograph, then."

Arthur was used to people talking about him in his presence as if he couldn't hear. It made him feel as if he were a television set. The man long-sufferingly tore apart a paper bag for him to autograph, shoved it onto his hand, and said furiously, "Haven't you even got anything to write with?" Arthur's affability began to be tinctured with a faint new sarcasm. He asked them into Sainsbury's, borrowed a pencil from the sausage assistant, and wrote his name on the paper bag.

"Phoney writing," the man said severely.

"What?" said his girl, leaning over his shoulder to look.

"I said phoney, not funny. I haven't laughed at him for years."

Arthur bought two pints of Devonshire cream as an act of aggression. Life being what it is, he thought, one dreams of revenge. He came out into the sun and wondered what next. Defend myself! I'm fed up with my place. I'd like a cat. A man must have somewhere to go.

Then he saw a wonderfully pretty girl who had obviously been watching him for a long time. It was Sukie, Sukie

something, the nymphet Fred was working with; he knew
her by the Afghans.

"You were even cooler than Fred," she said, laughing at
him admiringly and leaning her two dogs against her as if
they were supporting a fine book. He was glad she thought
he had been cool. He decided not to wipe his face, which
had started to run in its usual sleepy-fruit way, because to
do so might have destroyed the impression.

"Come home and have a drink," she said. "You're not
playing tonight, are you?" She imparted her knowledge of
him so agreeably, and her kneecaps looked so trustworthy,
that the glancingly unkind afternoon improved out of all
recognition. He had an obscure faith that he was in the
presence of some tributary of Fred's staunch temperament.
They walked to her car: two lean and amazing dogs, one
lean and amazing girl, and the old bladdery wineskin. Oh,
well. Oh, hell. She bought a choc-bar ice-cream on the
way, and this immediately gave him the illusion of proxy
licence that he always felt upon seeing the thin and flawless
elude the rules. Indeed, he even had a buccaneering moment
when it seemed to him that to have a choc-bar himself
would do the trick of making him exactly like her. So he
bought one. Her car was a red MG with the hood down,
parked closely; there was room for her to get in, but not for
him. She realized this openly and laughed at him in the sun,
saying that the Afghans couldn't manage it either, and her
blatant flirtatiousness fuelled him to perform one of his
music-hall leaps over the back of the car into the bucket seat.

"Fred never told me you did that sort of thing."

"I don't usually. Not in private life."

"He said you were shy. Do it again." She really was a

child. OK: one more when we get home and that's all before bedtime, he thought, facing the fact that bedtime was probably all too literally what she had in mind. Well, in that case, he told himself, there are ways of quieting kids down. Meaning no when you say it, for instance, and hot-milk drinks.

"Not here," he said maturely. "I'll do you one more when we get to your place." Her chin was shaped like a baby's heel.

She gave him a Coke out of a fridge that held caviare, half-empty tins of sardines and water-chestnuts, and medicine bottles for the dogs. There was also a cold-cream jar containing marijuana jam. The drawing-room was full of rugs that looked upsettingly as if they had been made from earlier Afghans. She sat on one of the longest-haired mats, draped the dogs around her, and catechized him about Fred with an insistence that he took for childishness. He tried asking her about herself, but she had a knack of averting his questions with an apparently bashful stammer, looking at him with kohl-lined eyes that rolled around like the globules in a bricklayer's balance. Her beauty was so startling that it mysteriously approached the comic. Arthur found the reasons for this unfathomable, but took it that they had to do with a comparison to his own looks. The sight of her bare toes made him feel slightly religious. When she wanted not to reply to something, she would lift her ravishing upper lip over her opened teeth in a way that put him alarmingly in mind of a horse wanting to be bridled. He grew very hot and thought that he was probably looking runnier than ever, but felt it would be courting horse trouble to take off his jacket. She was wearing schoolboy shorts herself, and what seemed to be an eleven-year-old's prep-school cricket blazer. Her hair was in a single pigtail tied with black bow, like one of Nelson's sailors. Merely to connect her with the Battle of Trafalgar liquefied him a little further because it moved him. He assumed the pigtail to be her own, but it wasn't. When she came back from changing, her haircut was a boy's, except that it had new-born-looking curls at the nape of her neck, which knocked him out for a bit. He went into her giant bathroom to take his mind off things and stood there awhile between her mirrors, thinking not particularly of how he looked himself but mostly of the inflections that she had caught from Fred, and also of how it must feel to be this negligently perfect child, who had obviously never in her life spent herself combating a flaw.

"You shouldn't wear a switch, you know," he said when he came back. "Your own hair's nicer."

"It's fun, that's all. It's boring to be the same all the time."

"When you're as pretty as you are, you should leave yourself alone."

She wavered her eyes at him, but he wasn't going to hand her anything more, for she knew perfectly well she was pretty. Not that her vanity took away from her; in some eerie way that he didn't relish, her self-absorption even made her harder to withstand. He found himself thinking solemnly about her bone structure, going on and on about it in his head, but put a stop to that because his thoughts sounded like the conversation of fashion photographers.

"Promise me not to wear a switch again," he said, after a fool's pause.

"Why? That's the whole *point* of living now. We can change ourselves. We can be anyone we want." She read too much newsprint, perhaps. "I've got dozens of wigs. I suppose you think that's frivolous of me. But I get so bored with myself. Don't you? What I mean is, you can choose now in the mornings whether you're going to be Marie Antoinette or a plumber's mate. As far as your hair's concerned, I mean. Or you can learn something. Like, er, Spanish. Anything. Shorthand. You can decide to have kids or not. You can be fat or thin. You just have to know what you want. Of course, it doesn't matter for a man about being fat. Women don't mind that sort of thing in men. I'd kill myself if I was fat." She poured a glass of Perrier water for herself and asked if he would like to smoke some pot. "If I was fat I simply couldn't stand it."

He watched her as she moved around the room. She was smoking her joint with quick snatches of breath, like a swimmer doing the crawl. He forgot for a moment that it was pot and thought of nicotine, and then of cancer, cells in delirium, the inroads that living would make one day even on this varnished little icon of the exempt: the flab of tiredness, children, overwork, sitting up too late at night listening to people, indulging buoyant childish appetites as a device to sustain good nature against foreshadows of the senile self.

"I hate Daisy, don't you?" said the little beauty, sitting cataclysmically on his knee, with a baby sparkle hard to tell from old-age mischief.

He put his huge right hand on her polished gold knee-caps, because it suddenly looked ridiculous lying around on the arm of a chair, and said, "No."

"Tell me about Fred. No. Tell me later, when we're in bed. I'll cook us some shepherd's pie. I'm a super cook. Did you know that? Fred told me you used to have shepherd's pie three or four times a week when you were in music hall. He said you liked it best the way they did it in Derby. Fred's a smashing man, isn't he? He's taught me everything. I even feel I know all about you. I mean, I know about your mother the harpist, and your father, and why you're called Arthur, and about the way you can fall. I wasn't really surprised when you jumped into the car like that, you know. I wanted you to." She was a witch, then, because he had never before in his life done such a thing with a girl in the street. She must have put the idea into his head herself: pinned it onto the back of his mind, like one of her flaming hairpieces.

The room was full of photographs of her. He looked at them. There was one of her dandling a baby, and he took it into the kitchen to her.

"It's my godchild," she said. "I adore babies. I'm going to have eight."

He looked at the backs of her knees, nearly fainted with the beauty of them, and went into the drawing-room again to convalesce, holding the photograph on his big lap. What was she doing? He couldn't see his way. He seemed to have become her creature, though she was the one on a drug supposed to make her passive. The cadences of Fred in her speech were cruelly deluding. She struck him as perilous and avid, and he had the sensation of going into a skid. He looked again at the photograph, and recognized at last that the baby who looked familiar was Fred's. No, Daisy's, with the child in the kitchen as her surrogate mother.

"How on earth did you get this?" he said. "It's Daisy's kid."

"I want Fred to see it." She smiled gaily, and a freezing wind howled in his guts.

"You need locking up."

"We'd better get on with it if you're going to be nasty, hadn't we? What a waste of my beautiful cooking. Still, I'm not really hungry. Are you?" She came and kissed him like an anteater, and he went out of the door. "You're frightened of me, aren't you?" she shrieked at him. "Come on, we could have fun. I think you're nice. I think you're attractive." He went down the stairs, and she stood at the top of them screaming. "I admire your work. Help, I'm falling."

"Hang on to the doorpost, then." He hesitated. She had certainly gone ashen, but it was probably pique. "Go to sleep," he said. "Have something to eat and go to sleep. It was a bad idea, that's all. And leave Fred and Daisy alone."

"I'll kill myself."

As soon as he got home, the telephone was ringing and she told him the same thing many times. "I'll kill myself."

"Where did you get my number?"

"From Fred."

"What've you done to him?"

"I'll kill myself if you don't come back."

"Eat your nice shepherd's pie and lay off. I've got to work tomorrow."

"So I'll never see you again."

"All right, I'll take you out to lunch one day."

"You don't love me. Mine's Flaxman 9424. You grab what you can get and then you desert me."

"Don't talk such bollocks. We've only just met."

"I can't bear being deserted. I won't have it. You're just like Fred. If you don't come back I'll take the whole bottle."

"You mean you did this to *Fred*."

"I can't stand it—I'm taking them—I'm giving them to the dogs. . . ."

She made her voice fade and left the receiver knocking against a table leg. Arthur listened carefully and heard her tiptoeing away. An hour later he dialled the number, but it was still engaged. The night seemed the longest he had endured. He sat for many hours in front of a mirror, moving his joints, detecting stiffness in a knee, juggling with cakes of soap to see if he could still do it. He was rehearsing Sir Toby Belch in *Twelfth Night* and the lines had fled; what he hung on to was the physical business, and when he did some of it to the mirror it seemed poor stuff for the old Living Boomerang. "I am not doing what I ought to do," he kept saying to himself. Was Fred free of that girl? He tried to reach her again, and told the operator to put the howler on the line because the phone was off the hook, but the girl said reprovingly that it couldn't be done in the middle of the night in case it woke people up. "It might be an emergency," Arthur said, though he didn't believe it. Then he got out his old square-toed athlete's shoes and practised falls onto the bed. His heart seemed to be beating too hard, and he started to test his twenty-twenty eyesight by leaping with alternate eyes closed. He thought the right one seemed weak. Perhaps it was tiredness. *I am not doing what I ought to do.*

The next day the press was onto him. Sukie had been rushed to hospital after taking an overdose of sleeping tablets, and she had left an incriminating love letter to him. It was printed next Sunday in one of the gutter tabloids. There were also photographs of himself, and of her bedroom as the police and reporters had found it, with the two Afghans poisoned on the floor.

Sukie recovered, and there were no charges to be brought, but she was a favoured public child as well as a minor and something stuck. After he opened in *Twelfth Night*, Arthur was hissed by a crowd of women waiting for him outside the stage door. It happened again, out of the blue, a few days later in Oxford Street. He thought of something he had read once about Fielding, who had heard the watermen at Rotherhithe mocking his body when it had grown ugly with the dropsy.

Fred understood Sukie's vengeful ruse, and most people could have guessed it if they had cared to, which they didn't. Often it isn't the truth that punishes but what's believed. After a fortnight, Fred saw what was likely to happen and went to a lawyer whom he trusted. "The girl's practically a nut. Can't he make a statement?"

"It'll do more harm than good."

"You think it'll die down?"

The lawyer looked out the window. "You know what I really think? His weight will damn him. He'll become a monster."

Arthur survived. Defeat was too great a compliment to pay to society. He merely changed. He started to smoke incessantly, carrying around a cigarette box as big as a biscuit tin. He lost so much weight that he wore two suits, one on top of the other, because he despised the sign of toll.

I'm the kind you can trample for a time.
But then I quit.
God hear,
That's it.

He woke up in the middle of some night with this composed in his head. He had practically no money left in the world, but he went on drinking champagne on credit. After he had been out of work for months his telephone rang and a manager asked to see him. In his office the manager said that he thought he might have a part going, and then looked at Arthur for a long time. Arthur looked back grimly. "No," the manager said. "It isn't for you. But keep in touch." Arthur left without a word. What had he been expected to do? Go down on his knees?

Fred was killed in a car crash at the end of the year. By that time Arthur had started again as near as possible to the place where he had begun. He played in working-men's clubs in the North of England. They didn't pay much, but they were more like the old music halls than anything left in the South. With an enjoyment that came back as soon as he started to work, he invented a solo routine that was deliberately and taxingly physical. The audiences at the first show of the evening were sparse but hair-raisingly alert. The second houses were packed, but the people were generally too drunk to pay much attention. The roaring, boozing Saturday nights were always great.

Daisy found him by telephone in Harrogate with the news of Fred's death and asked him to identify the body for her. She seemed to be asking not so much to save herself as because of some instinct for the men's friendship. Arthur flew to London and stayed in the police morgue a long time with the body that he knew as closely as his own, thinking of Fred's splendid good nature, his tough-mindedness, and his humour about the absurd and even the terrible. Daisy let Arthur pay for the funeral, although she knew he had no money. His choices were old-fashioned and lavish, with a full choir and more flowers than he could possibly afford. The bills came on the morning of the burial, and he suddenly drew them from his pocket during the service, opening them without knowing what he was doing. He crushed them in his hand as he passed the coffin and shouted at the lid, weeping, "Even when you're dead you cost me too much."

Living on the Box

The poet, feeling stale, thought the world stale and began to abuse it. Since he lived in isolation, being a nature poet and finding contact with people a digression from his work, the only object of abuse that was readily available to him was his wife.

During the twelve years of their life together, he had tutored her carefully in monkishness. As part of the training he spoke to her rarely. To rail at her meant opening a conversation, and this involved preposterous changes in his day.

Generally he rose at five-thirty, before she was awake. She got up later than he did because she went to sleep later, tossing and sometimes weeping, and in the end usually fumbling her way downstairs to get herself a drink. Until noon he stayed out of the cottage, walking across the Northumbrian moors with a knob-headed stick and humming Anglican hymns, whose verbal schemes he admired for their metrical embodiment of depression. At twelve he had a simple meal, cooked with natural foods and sea salt, which she hacked with a chisel from a damp sackful in the yard. At one he slept, and at three he worked in a shed at the bottom of the garden. In the evenings they read together, keeping silent because he believed that silence was more real than chatter, and at half past nine they went to bed. Sometimes she sat on the end of his divan if she couldn't sleep and tried to wake him up to talk, but he slept with the heaviness of the very thin, and her weight on the divan made it sag and creak in a way that embarrassed her.

In the earlier years of living with her he had sometimes left her a note speared on the kitchen tap before he went out for his walk—stirred and perhaps even drawn by the sight of her plain, flushed face in bed, which had begun to acquire in sleep a look of distress and disappointment. Lately the notes had not been written. She thought the zest of her replies probably struck him as crude. In his mordant presence she always felt vulgar and self-indulgent. When he made one of his rare, shapely jokes, they gave her a flash of great pleasure—a passing reassurance that life was good after all—and then an experience of despair and palsy. He was the only person she had ever known whose humour seemed entirely immobile. It expressed no wish, no venom, no energy in any direction. But to complain that its effect was therefore paralysingly glum would no more have occurred to her as fair than to complain that it made her feel fat. It did both, but this only drove home to her the grossness and subjectivity of her own temperament. On an evening when he had broken the silence with one of his quietist cracks she would feel a sense of remorse and insufficiency descending on her, and hours later find herself in the larder, eating the remains of whatever was under the meat sieve and weeping that she should do something so self-defeating and stupid.

On the days when he used to leave her a note in the morning she knew well enough that there was no good to be hoped for in replying to it. She understood that her excitement upset his sense of style. At the same time she was so ravenous to talk to him that it was quite impossible to stop herself. She would write her first reply in the bathroom, turning on the geyser to pretend she was having a bath and writing joyfully on a breadboard balanced on the small wooden basin (they used a breadboard as a bathmat on the freezing floor, because he liked the genuineness of natural wood). And then, after putting the note on his bed for him to read when he came back for his rest and covering it with the undyed hessian bedspread in case their child saw it, she would sit down and try to wring words out of the sleepy little boy at breakfast before he went off to school, and find that she had an empty morning in which to worry about what she had written. She would make the poet's lunch, starting with the radio playing but switching it off after a time because he believed that people should be able to do without background noise. And as she was moving about she would realize that her letter communicated nothing of her pleasure and love, so she would get the paper back and add a postscript and a laborious drawing. Then she would do housework, but it was such an austere cottage that there was hardly anything to do. And while she was having a whisky and eating a piece of cake at eleven o'clock, in a hapless impulse to demonstrate and somehow fix her freebooting mood—though she saw the irrationality of it on a day that had begun with a clear insight that at least she would try to equal his thinness even if she could never hope to achieve the frugality of his expectations—just as she was leaving the last part of the cake, she would think of a better way to write the note. By the time she had done it several times, and copied out the post-script, and redone the drawing, it sounded false to her and she lost her nerve completely. At lunchtime, when he read the note, he would always thank her as warmly as he could, but her mistake of taste was plainly defined in his face.

She had a vision of him sometimes, struggling for breath beneath the crassness of her impulses, in the same way that she sometimes imagined her fattening body to be asphyxiating his small fine frame in bed. Shy and unhappy, she one day went to sleep in the spare room, hoping that he would come in to find her, but he credited her with his own temperament and thought only that she wished to be alone. Indeed, he was quite unaware of her frenzy and mildly loved her.

The absurd fact was that he had married her for her gaiety. But in his grey presence her larks had soon seemed shameful, and she had disciplined herself as though she were entering an order. He observed the ebbing of her vivacity with thoughtless disappointment. Occasionally he hated her for it, because he took it to be a reproach of himself. Their life was one for which she was very unfitted, and her gigantic effort to enjoy it struck him as a piece of self-deception. He knew, when he considered the point, that she did not even really like his poetry. His visions of moral order in biology and of the superior integrity of sap, expressed in a thin, precise style like the print of a hopping bird in snow, struck her as impossible to live with. But, on the face of it, the perfect little couplets about twigs and foxes that he wrung out of his gargantuan walks justified the form of their lives as fully in her eyes as in his. She knew everything he had written by heart. The sound of her repeating a line back at him drove him mad.

"Have some more stew," she said one evening.

"No thank you."

"Is anything the matter?"

"No."

"Is work all right?"

He didn't reply, and filled his pipe. She came round to his chair and put her big arms around his neck, aware of what her flesh would feel like on his skin and at the same time ashamed to be self-conscious. "I was thinking today about 'Frost'," she said. Unable to see his face, she recited "Frost" to him. Her voice was pretty, but she made "Frost" sound a thin dirge, and he looked murderous. He decided at that moment to make a victim of her.

One morning, he stayed at home and dropped his gum boots hard beside her bed to wake her up.

"You'd rather I wrote sea shanties," he said in her ear.

She looked alarmed. "What time is it?"

"Or hornpipes."

"Why haven't you gone out today? Have you got a cold?"

"You'd like it better if I tried to make people happy, wouldn't you? What obligation have I to do that? Or to you, to make you happy? Doesn't it ever strike you as faintly ludicrous—the pursuit of happiness by a species that is less equipped for it than anything in nature?" He did a short angry dance by the bed. It was like the rollicking of a Desert Father.

"I don't understand a word you're saying."

"Naturally."

"I've only just woken up."

"I wish you wouldn't deceive yourself."

"What about?"

"How unhappy you are. How much you hate my poetry."

"I don't. I love it. You. . . . I don't understand."

"You aren't asked to."

"But we live together."

"We might be on other planets."

"I thought you liked being left on your own."

"On my own? I'm about as much on my own here as a man with a dog that wants to be taken for a walk. Your forbearance is a weapon that you know how to use all too well."

She started to weep, with her long brown hair falling over her face.

"Don't. You look like Elizabeth Barrett Browning's spaniel with a cold," he said thinly.

Later there was a letter from the BBC about doing a long television interview. Out of waywardness, because she had assumed he wouldn't want to, he decided to accept.

"It'll certainly be a coup for them," she said helplessly. In extremity, she kept trying to be pleasant. "I expect you'd like me out of the road. Though perhaps they'll want lunch."

"They'll be here all day. They're sure to want the poet's wife," he said tartly. "You can tell them how much you love the work, can't you?" He always spoke about his poetry as "the work"; it was this sort of dispassion that so excited the BBC.

"We must get all this!" cried the young producer to his assistant, driving his Rover over the moors from Newcastle and pointing to the horizon. "Somehow the sky seems bigger up here. I think one feels that in his poetry."

"We mustn't force the domestic part of it in this one," the assistant said. "I'm not sure we shouldn't do it all outside. What do you think? He's such an abrasive spirit, isn't he? Nothing . . . upholstered—do you know what I mean? That's what so remarkable about him."

"I suppose he's one of the few classicists writing. Is that the line, do you think? One could say that he was the dissenter in an age of . . . romantic anarchy. Anarchic romanticism. No. Megalopolitan romanticism, perhaps. Anyway, an age with an intense admiration for disorder. Whereas he sees *order* in things, doesn't he? In a very unfashionable way."

The poet's wife was told when they arrived that they would want to film her. She had spent too long getting dressed, changing again and again, because her thighs looked bigger in every pair of trousers that she put on. The exertion and self-scrutiny had made her flush, and she began to turn purple under layers of powder. This made her late with the lunch, and at the table she found the young men impossible to talk to because she was trying to retain the lines of what she had prepared to say. In the afternoon, they went out on the moors with the cameras, and she sat crouched over the plates while the logic of the sentences fell apart completely. She wanted to talk about his poetry. All she could think of was the two of them, and her suspicion that he was right about her. She knew that she had never been an intellectual, but she thought that she had probably once been capable of insight. At the beginning she had known clearly enough that he was an irrevocably solitary man, and it had seemed to her fortunate to live with him at all. He would say, "People need air round them," and she would pretend she agreed. Or perhaps she had felt it then herself.

When the young men came back and started to film her in the kitchen, she forgot every word she had learned.

The poet had no television. To watch the programme, a month later, they went with their child to Newcastle and took a room at the Station Hotel. The poet's wife tried to avoid going, by saying that it was late for the child and that she would have expected her husband not to be curious. While they waited in the room, which was furnished like a nursing home, with the child reading a comic on the bed and eating a bag of shortbread biscuits, she thought that it was as well to be next door to the railway station in case she had to get away quickly.

At the sight of his big-nosed face slanted across the screen, like a pale and captious parrot, the poet detested his sufficiency and looked across at her to ward off its effect. He had a powerful impression that the programme was happening in a vault. When the film used some footage of his wife moving about the cottage, he felt as if he had been given a reprieve. She used this moment to light a cigarette.

"What's 'Muse'?" the child asked suddenly.

"Shut up," his mother said.

"Father keeps saying it."

"It's what I hang around for all day," said the poet, "when your mother is doing something useful."

"Useful! You could do without any of it. And what do you mean, that you hang around? You write on the dot. Nothing stops you. It's like the bloody crops."

"I can't hear," the child said.

"If some people think that I live in a void, as you put it," said the poet on television, "perhaps that tells us more about them than about me. I can't think of a thousand acres of natural activity as a void. I agree that it's not a particularly easy life for most people to support. I don't suppose my wife finds it easy, for example. But for me it's the condition of working. I find most company the opposite of useful, because it's conducted at a feverish level. The high temperature of the modern is what I suspect most about it. Art now romanticizes chaos. We have developed an aesthetic of inconsequence and accident. I mistrust a literature that finds suicide more significant than death, and a man's inability to communicate more sorry than the frenzy of his need to. By celebrating the clamorous, we celebrate the bomb."

The poet's wife turned away her head and tried to grow absorbed in their child.

"Twentieth-century art glamorizes the act of flying apart," the poet on television continued. "No one seems to face the fact that this is bound to reduce the tragic to the simply catastrophic. There's nothing tragic about a man flying off course like a burst tyre and exploding in a ditch. We now have a colossal documentation of what it feels like to be in the margin. The sensibility of the centrifugal can't go any further, can it? It can only become more heated. Or as I see it, more sentimental. It seems to me that there is something finally maudlin and trivial about seeing neurosis as Nemesis."

The camera shifted angle: white face against white wall, a head picked clean of expression, like a skull. The poet felt indifferent toward it; the poet's wife felt suddenly free of it.

"Not that I find it easy to deny what everyone else in Europe apparently finds truthful. But I should like to make poems that are about space and order, in the same sense as some modern sculpture. Not poems that make you feel on the *edge* of space but poems that make you feel you contain space *inside yourself*. I've seen abstracts that do this. With the verbal arts I think it can only be done for the moment by writing about nature. In an age that sees all human behaviour and motive as finally hectic, and finds an art that says so rather glorious, the humanist is driven to the vegetable."

The poet's wife unexpectedly laughed. "You never said all this."

"I thought it was implicit."

"I hadn't any idea you would call yourself a humanist."

". . . not a *void*, anyway. Simply to contain space," said the television in the poet's voice, over a shot of him half an inch high striding over the moors. "The word 'void' only projects modern people's irritation with anyone outside their own trap. I expect my wife used it."

The poet hadn't expected the programme to leave this in, and he was shocked.

"He doesn't live in a void," said the poet's wife on television, in a cut that shook her with its glibness.

They had photographed her sitting on a kitchen stool in a white passage, with her back against a long stretch of wall, like someone at a dance. "'Void' is the wrong word. He lives in a sort of gavotte where no one is ever going to drop a glove. But he calls it a world, and he's such a good writer that he can make it seem like one. I think he feels that the most difficult thing in a man's life is to find some sort of balance between longing for company and longing for isolation. Some of us don't think of that till we're dying. My husband has been practising dying for years. I never know whether the death wish is a wish to get out of activity or out of existence. My husband said once that he wanted to be dead but still to be. I don't understand that. I'm a poor person to talk about his work really, because I don't understand the open air. But looking for the truth in nature walks? Hips and haws don't *mean* anything. They're just hips and haws. He thinks a tide chart is a sort of hymn sheet. The only difference between the significance of a tide chart and the significance of a railway timetable is that a railway timetable can be altered, isn't it? I don't believe that the sort of intractability there is in nature has very much to teach us. I think it just excites people now because it's remote, like the idea of four days of lemon juice to men who have business lunches every day. I mean ... I suppose I mean that I don't think my husband would be a nature poet if he didn't live now, here, in England. Some other time, he might have been a hymn writer, perhaps. Or a theologian. He just has a monkish temperament. I make it sound as if he finds it easy. . . . He doesn't really dislike people. He used to love girls. I think his poetry is an effort to be stoic. Being married is probably a hindrance."

"You shouldn't have said that," said the poet.

She watched her big face fade into a still of his Savon-arola profile while an actorish voice spoke more of his verse.

"Did you expect them to leave all that in?" he said.

"I suppose so."

"You talked as if I were dead. Or deaf."

"No. I'd never, never have said such things if you were dead." She wondered how she could explain this to him if he didn't see it already. The little boy had lost interest and started pulling open the drawers of the dressing-table. She put her coat on.

"You looked beautiful," he said after a pause that agonized them both. He was suddenly moved by her physically, as he had been by the sight of her in the film. "Like a Bonnard."

She thought he was throwing her a sop and it steeled her.

"I'm sorry," she said stiffly.

"You should have said it all before."

"I didn't know it before."

"Other people would call it treacherous, I suppose. I don't. It's rather a relief. Where are you going?"

"London." She packed the child into his gum boots.

"Oh, no. Not now. It'll be all right. I'm not angry. It's absurd to go because you think I'm angry. Is that it?"

"I can't do anything else now. It's happened in the wrong order. Most things about us have. Not like botany at all."

She kept her face turned away as she moved about the room, and looked stony. At the door she suddenly grinned at him, and when she had gone the grin seemed to him still to be hanging in the air, like the Cheshire cat's. He wept.

*

That night he took a midnight train to London, searched for her all day, and had his first demanding quarrel with her in a Chinese restaurant at five o'clock in the afternoon, blue-jowled with fear and tiredness, and smelling of the stale smells of travellers. She came back to the north with him after that and they lived together again for a time.

The Tactics of Hunger

"Algy is a she!" Lady Grubb shouted into the telephone to the young man from Fleet Street. "The he is called Guy. It's quite clear which is which in *Burke's Peerage*. Surely you have *Burke's Peerage*?"

The gossip reporter said that he had, but she overrode him. "If your newspaper can't aff rd it, then go to the public reference library. There is one beside a cinematographic house in Leicester Square. But surely you should possess a copy. Tell your proprietor I said so."

Her twin children, bitterly cold, fiddled with their sherry, which had been mixed with whisky in the decanter by mistake, and took the reporter's side. "He's *got* a copy of it, Ma. He keeps telling you," said Algy, who was the girl, as her mother had bellowed.

Lady Grubb made a whirring noise like a pheasant going up. "Why didn't he say so?" She glared at the telephone dial as if it were the young man's face and held the receiver away from her ear. "What did you telephone for, then?" she said into the mouthpiece. "No, of course she's not engaged. She hasn't come *out* yet."

The fact was that Algy had been living for the last year with a working-class architect called Len in a basement flat in Maida Vale. But her mother, who was hostile to facts, had gone on entertaining for her as if she were a chaste child just emerging from school. The young men she rustled up as marriage candidates seemed to Algy to be all one person with different haircuts, well-born dullards on their way into industry who exclaimed "I say, how jolly enterprising!" when they heard that Algy was a scene painter, and who surprised her by still dancing foxtrots and rumbas that she thought extinct. This weekend she had finally braced herself to the course of obtruding the existence of Len into the house. She had thought for months of trying to blow the gaff on the fact that she was past marrying off, but it had seemed a lot to put Len through, and her mother was any-way exceptionally good at not acknowledging that a gaff had been blown.

At sixteen, three years ago, she and her brother had erupted together from home practically unnoticed. Their parents were elderly, though not as elderly as they seemed. Lady Grubb had fallen easily into the habit of behaving to her children as if she were some doggedly snobbish god-mother, inviting them home every few months to look into their marriage prospects and treating the occasion as if it were a country weekend that put her to a lot of trouble, though her house was actually in the middle of London and fully staffed with unhappy *au-pair* girls. Reality got through to her intermittently; her apprehension of it was uncommonly tuned, for though she was generally oblivious to the most apparent, she was often startled by things to which others were deaf. When Guy brought his girl friend home for the weekend, for instance, the air was thick with sex, but Lady Grubb noticed nothing. On the other hand, when she had taken up the carpets for a dance for Algy and filled the house with sixteen-year-old boys from Harrow and Marlborough, she twitched to the thin soprano signals of public-school lust like a dog hearing the squeak of a rat in its sleep. She was cruelly obsessed with class and if her children had not come from a background that she knew to be reliable she would certainly have ignored them as she ignored the *au-pair* girls.

"I wish she'd get her hair done," Algy said when Lady Grubb was out of the room.

"She looks all right," said her brother.

"No she doesn't. She used to be pretty."

"You're kidding yourself. When's Len coming?"

"Late as possible."

Lady Grubb's invitations to them were always by letter, and led to a file of correspondence because she enjoyed making microscopic changes of plan. The first summons habitually began with a long and belligerent explanation of why some other weekend was not possible. As it had never been proposed in the first place, her children could read this only as a piece of unadmitted defensiveness about having ignored them in the past. They dreaded the prospect of accepting, but they were fond of their father, so they generally packed warm clothes and went.

Lady Grubb kept the house miserably cold. Occasionally she recited, as though it were a rule of life, a testy saw of her own invention maintaining that fifty-five degrees Fahrenheit was the correct temperature for a drawing-room and fifty degrees for corridors and bedrooms. Bathrooms she regarded as outhouses. She was a clever woman with obscure sources of energy who would suddenly start to garden by torchlight late at night, or walk wilfully all the way to Soho to buy vegetables at the times when the pin in her hipbone was especially painful. In other moods she would go to bed for days, and have trays sent up to her room that were laden with stingy nursery snacks of mashed fish and junket. Her interests, when they were detectable, were urgent and surprising. Sometimes she startled her mild husband by knowing all about African politics. Lord Grubb was an ancient hereditary peer who kept up eagerly with the times and was trying at the moment to unlock his capital to set up a chain of waffle shops. His wife, more canny than she seemed, had already witnessed huge losses over a scheme to promote detachable shirt cuffs, and so far she had managed to sit on the remaining money. Lately he had been troubled by rheumatism brought on by the damp in the house, and his doctor had set him up in sleeping quarters on the ground floor with independent heating arrangements. But his bathroom was in the conservatory, which had two doors on to the garden where his wife grew plants, and as she left these doors open all morning his part of the house was apt to be colder than anywhere.

The house was decorated almost entirely in weedy shades of green and looked to the children like a fish tank that needed cleaning out. Lady Grubb knew a great deal about antiques and owned some beautiful pieces, but she topped up the genuine furnishings with reproduction Jacobean coffee tables and plastic cruets. The cruets were said to have been bought in the cause of saving the work of cleaning silver ones, but she still made the *au-pair* girls polish a hoard of Georgian silverware in the cellar every week. One of her hobbies was anæsthetics, and she subscribed to an anæsthetists' journal in which she had seen an advertisement for a chemist who outfitted doctors' waiting-rooms and surgeries. This had appealed to her, and recently she had replaced a broken standard lamp in the drawing-room with an operating arc light. It had been refitted with a low-watt bulb practically too dim to see by, in order to save electricity.

Algy particularly was made miserable by the change in the house. Her only pleasure in it now was the notes left all over the place by her father: cheery instructions in a classical scholar's hand, written on the gummed labels used by the more pious English government departments to get a second use out of old envelopes. "If this drawer sticks, don't despair," said a label on a Queen Anne chest in the spare room. "It will open if tugged sharply to the right." And on the bedside table, facing the sleeper: "Don't be alarmed by any irregular thudding noise in the night. It is probably the water tank. If in doubt, call for help." Lord Grubb knew well enough that Algy dreaded her visits, and to let her off the trial of breakfasting with her mother he had installed a complicated route of strings and pulleys that led from her second-storey bedroom to the basement. This made a placard spring out in the kitchen. It said, "I'm ready for breakfast. Thank you." The idea of a bell didn't occur to him.

"Ma must have taken to cooking up bits of food in her bedroom," Algy said when Lady Grubb was doing something to the plants and she and Guy were alone with father in his study.

"What do you mean?"

"She's got a Primus in there."

"I haven't been up for a while," her father said, implying a total absence of mind, and some of body, too.

"She seems extra loopy today."

"Eh?"

"I wish she wouldn't wear those cardigans," Guy said. "She looks like a Scripture mistress out to grass."

"When does she expect us to leave?" Algy said. "Lord, it's only Friday."

"I don't know, my darling," Lord Grubb said. "Whenever you like. Sunday evening?"

"Last time she couldn't wait to be rid of us. She didn't say a word all Sunday."

"I think she was frightened to ask how long you were staying in case you left," said Lord Grubb, with a lunge of shrewdness.

When Len arrived, they seemed for some reason to talk about nothing but health. He was a tall, shy, bony man with a stoop, who cracked his fingers when he was worried. He expected to be patronized by Lady Grubb because he came from a lower class, about which he didn't generally care tuppence, but when he saw her effect on Algy he found it more difficult than usual to be ribald about it.

"You've got a cold," Lady Grubb said accusingly to her son.

"No I haven't. I don't *think* I have, at least. Have I?"

"I can *always* tell when you have a cold," she said, brooking no argument. "The whites of your eyes go pink." Then she said to Len, but without turning to him, "Do you get ill much, Mr Warren?"

"Hardly ever."

"We've all had colds here. Cecil had a snorter. I could hear him honking all the way from my bedroom. He lives on the garden level because he suffers from gout."

"Rheumatism," Lord Grubb said softly.

"Did you know that tortoises get gout? If they're brought to a cold climate too young, that is. I persuaded our member of Parliament to introduce a bill about it. About the importation of small tortoises. One can judge the age by length."

"Daddy wouldn't have rheumatism if the house wasn't so damp," Guy said.

"The place isn't damp at all," said Lord Grubb. "You can always tell a damp house by the state of the cigars."

"It must be very different where you come from," Lady Grubb said enigmatically to Len, who came from Putney. Putney was two miles away at the most, but she implied that it was two thousand.

"I'm afraid this is what you'll have had every day of your life," she said to him later as the *au-pair* girl put a plate of mutton in front of him. Algy suddenly realized that her mother was engaged in an elaborate pretence that he was a New Zealander.

"Not a bit. Algy and I live off baked beans," Len said.

"Ma," Algy said, "Len was born in *Putney*."

Lady Grubb graciously ignored the rebuttals. "Would you like some ice in your drinking water?"

"Aren't you having wine?" Algy said to him.

"Don't press it on him," said Lady Grubb. "He's not accustomed to it. We had an American to dine the other day who wanted coffee with the sirloin."

"Len and I have wine all the time," Algy said, but facts led nowhere; they never had.

"Have you found somewhere pleasant to live in London?" Lady Grubb said.

"He lives with *me*, Ma. He's *always* lived in London."

"I expect you'd like to meet a few people. Algy must remember to ask you to come next time I give a little party for her. There are always plenty of spare girls."

The *au-pair* maid went down to the basement and again started plotting with her friend how soon they would have enough money for the fare home to Zurich. When she came in with the junket, the row had obviously developed. There was a V-shaped vein sticking out in Algy's forehead. Lady Grubb looked triumphant. Lord Grubb was trying to concentrate on taking the band off a cigar. Guy had left his mutton, and Len was watching Algy.

"Where on earth did that trolley come from, Ma?" she said.

"The chemist."

"You're furnishing the whole place from a medical outfitter. It's starting to look like an obstetrician's lumber room."

"It's not your house."

"It's certainly never felt like it. You're dead right."

"*Too* right, as your friend would say," Lady Grubb replied, imitating a New Zealand accent. "Will you have some junket? Louise makes it very nicely."

"You must have rennet spilling out of your ears," Algy said to Louise, who by now was beyond taking pleasure in such moves of friendliness and simply handed round the dish with her left hand behind her back as she had been taught, feeling mutinous and thinking proudly of a home-land where not junket but fondue was the commonplace.

"*Why* do you shop at the chemist's?" Algy said to her mother, stupidly pursuing the question of the trolley.

"I had to go there anyway and I saw it. I needed some things as presents." Her children knew at once the sort of things that these would be. Last year for Christmas she had given Louise a red rubber medical bathmat for the aged.

There was a silence, and then Lady Grubb said, "It was quite a pleasant walk."

"But why couldn't you telephone? They deliver."

"The delivery is very unreliable."

"Oh, Ma. The one thing that chemists are is reliable. That's what their profession is. Like those men in long white overalls who see schoolchildren across the road."

"Last week they made a mistake on a prescription label."

"Well," Algy said lightly, "don't be a nit—complain to the *Lancet*. Or go to another chemist."

"'Nit' must be a local word that you taught her?" Lady Grubb said to Len.

Dislike ran round the table like electricity, and the lightning generated and struck. "Come off it, you old bag," Len said. "I'm not that outlandish. I was born two miles away. My mum probably did your scrubbing."

Then it was as if trees started crashing down and roots tearing out of the ground. Algy began abusing her mother. Lord Grubb, in terror, waved his arthritic right hand at Algy with a patting motion of great violence and scattered cigar ash on his beautiful old green smoking jacket. "Don't rise to it, sweetheart!" he shouted. "Don't you see your mother's only trying to convince herself your friend doesn't belong here?"

"Don't you think it's time she realized he did?" Algy said coldly.

"Probably," said her father. "But she's old. We're both old. I hate her. She's going to die first and she won't notice it, and then I'll be on my own. It's not dying I'm afraid of; it's being dead."

Lady Grubb picked up her plate of junket and went to eat it in the drawing-room, shaking with a passion she didn't care to scrutinize because it contained not only fury but also amazement and fear.

"She's killing herself with what she eats," said Lord Grubb to the three left at the table, who felt they should be listening to nothing. "It's not fair. It's not fair to me. I don't want to be on my own. One more fall and she'll break her hip again and then she'll die. What she puts into her system isn't fit for a woman of her age. It's pap. It's food for premature lambs. But she won't do anything I say. I might as well not exist. I write her notes every day—notes all over the house, in her potting shed, and on her food lift. I try to warn her and she pays no attention. She never replies. Sometimes I think she can't read any longer. For all she advises me of her condition she might be *blind* and I wouldn't know it. I hate her. I've written her notes and notes and notes and she's never answered one of them. Surely she could send me a message of some sort? She's only to give an envelope to Louise. I haven't seen her handwriting for so long that I can hardly remember what it's like. Perhaps she can't even hold a pen any longer. Perhaps she can't do *anything* any longer. Poor soul. Poor old cocky. She used to call me 'my old mate' when she was a girl, you know. It was a joke from a music-hall song. I hate the sight of her now. She's nearly dead. I know it."

"Father," Guy said. Then he could find nothing more to say at all. It was impossible to find any landmarks for the moment. The balance of power had moved like the contours of a desert after a night wind. What was happening? Before this, the twins' visits had always seemed extorted. Now it was apparently neither here nor there that the two even happened to be present. They had always written off their mother's manœuvres as tribal tactics devised to keep the two of them for her kind, with their father as some sort of lower ally in the endeavour, more deeply absorbed by his autonomy and his cigars than by the dynamics of living with his wife. But now his needs seemed more urgent and primal than hers.

"You mean she won't admit she's ill?" Algy said.

"That's what he's been saying all the time," said Len. "Haven't you been listening? Lord Grubb says she won't admit anything. Blimey, she wouldn't even admit I'm English."

"Oh, shut up. Of *course* I've been listening," Algy said to Len. "I can't get . . ." She waited and tried again, to her father. "You mean she's frightened of the doctor and she thinks you're going to send for him behind her back?"

"You can't possibly be suggesting Father *intimidates* her," Guy said. "Not Mamma."

"She won't confess it," Lord Grubb said, hectoring the table but still powerfully giving the impression of talking *sotto voce* to himself. "She's blind, for all I know, and half starved. Probably even all those long walks she says she takes are a pretence to put me off. It's quite likely she calls a taxicab every time and has it waiting round the corner out of sight. It's perfectly probable she can't even get *about* now. I write to her about it again and again."

"You keep talking as if you live in different houses," Algy said.

"She's going to die, and she's keeping it from me. She was always secretive. I won't stand for it. She's got to put it in writing."

"Do you want me to talk to her?" Guy said. "If you're as worried as this. . . . But she doesn't seem ill. That's what I don't understand. Does she, Algy? And if she is, surely she's perfectly capable of calling a doctor herself. Isn't she?"

"She does it to spite me," his father said. "Don't you see what I'm saying? She refuses to answer. I never hear from her."

"Daddy, you *live together*," Algy said.

"Talk to her when we've gone and tell her that *we're* going to get a doctor to come. Would that make it easier?" Guy said.

Lord Grubb snorted and looked sulky. The room was full of ire.

Len said carefully, "When my dad died, he and my mum hadn't spoken for three years. They'd had a fight." He watched, on an instinct. The block of paranoia sitting at the other end of the table minutely shifted shape.

"I certainly shan't speak to her until she starts replying to my letters," said Lord Grubb, cued in so that it was possible to say it at last.

*

Algy got up from the table and went into the drawing-room. After a moment Len followed her.

"Ma," Algy said, as normally as possible. "Is it true that you and Daddy don't talk to each other?"

Lady Grubb suddenly wept over the magazine on her lap and the finished plate of junket. It was a spasm, over at once, like a sneeze. "My hip hurts," she said.

"You can't go on like this," Algy said.

"My mum and dad managed not to open their traps to each other for fourteen years," Len said. "Mum used to play the wireless and turn on all the bath taps as soon as he came in. Even in front of me they did it. At least you two don't do that." He tried a cliché, to seem breezy. "There's always somebody worse off than yourself."

"It's the only time I hear his voice, when you two come," Lady Grubb said, "He even leaves notes for the maids."

"Do *you* speak to *him*?" Algy said.

"I won't be bullied. Why should one? Getting nagging letters in one's own house. During the Labour landslide they used to be *love* letters. He hasn't even changed his handwriting. It's perfidy. Even the same black ink. Reminding and reminding me. He's trying to break into me."

"Which Labour landslide?" Len said softly.

"Ramsay MacDonald's."

"Why don't you speak to him?" Algy said, sitting on a low tapestry footstool by her mother's chair and putting her forefinger on Lady Grubb's big garnet ring as if she were pressing a doorbell, staring up at the implacable old head and thinking of nothing but of how to get her to look at one of the two people in the room.

"He's going to die," said Lady Grubb, eyes fixed on the

carpet. "He'll die first and he knows it. Then I'll be on my own. I have to practise being on my own."

"Is that why he moved downstairs? To make you learn? I thought it was because of his gout."

"You silly goose. The young guess nothing."

"If you mean about being lonely . . ." Len said. "If you mean we don't know much about being alone because we don't find it difficult, that's true."

"No one understands loneliness if they haven't been married," Lady Grubb said. "For forty years. . . . You two. Fly-by-night affairs. You risk nothing."

Algy turned on Len. "It's not true at all. Do you really think I don't know what isolation's like? What do you imagine goes on in my head all night when you've been talking about splitting up? You hope it takes the pain out of it to talk about it, but it doesn't. You said when we bought those bloody birds last Christmas, 'I wonder how long it'll be before we're yanking all this apart again and halving the furniture and carving up the doves.' I've never forgotten it. It's unbearable."

"Oh, come on," Len said. "Not unbearable. Inevitable. When it happens it'll just happen naturally, and that's all there'll be to it. It would be silly for us to say *if* it happens, because it's bound to. The things you can't avoid are the easy part."

"I see," Algy said angrily. "Like dying."

Albert

Terror of the next move. Albert Cruikshank, customs officer at London Airport, had told his wife, Bella, that he knew she was in love with his best friend. There had been an anonymous telephone call to tell him so, but he had guessed it anyway, mostly because her habit of reversing the responsibility for everything that happened had made her start to behave as though she had herself some gross cause for mistrust. His jokes with her had started jamming, and she had grown steely and even gone through his pockets. There was something obscurely over-energized about her, quite unlike his old succulently lazy wife, and she had begun to clean the house as if it were a sin of the flesh.

"Come and sit with me," he had called one night.

"I was lying in the bath," she had said, marching downstairs with a towel draped round her, looking ravishing but severe about the face. "There's a brown rim under the soapdish!" she shouted from the kitchen, coming back with a scrubbing brush and abrasives. "You can see it quite clearly when you're lying down." He had thought she must be joking, but she wasn't. The change in her left him helpless. In the next few days she had kept speaking of their child as "my son", with a possessiveness that struck him as bestial and prescient.

As soon as he confessed what he knew, fumbling the hideous admission as they came out of a rather good film about love that he had hardly been able to stand, she managed to make it seem that it was he, not she, who was the disturber of their lives. If he hadn't brought it up, she said resentfully again and again, everything would still have been the same. The anarchy of her action was apparently his, for knowing of it.

Contact between them was immediately ignoble. She went on seeing Jim, his friend, his appalled good friend, just as before—perhaps even in his own bed, Albert realized, since the shift-work timing of a customs officer's job made the logistics of adultery comically easy. He took this in suddenly one morning as he was charging a girl the duty on a camera, hitting the thought like an air pocket and ludicrously yawning at the same time with his mouth shut so that the girl noticed his face lengthening like a mule's. When he tried to talk to Bella in bed at night, there were passing moments of ease and sweetness that made it seem almost possible to recover what had been lost. And then they would start wrangling, and she would shout that he was keeping her awake and fall asleep while he listened for hours to her breathing; and next morning reprisals would be exacted for her fatigue.

After a week he walked out, suddenly, with their five-year-old son. He left a meticulously explanatory note on her dressing-table to say that he and the child would be telephoning, and went to ground at the airport hotel. It was Friday. He had three days off. Now what? He didn't telephone. He sat in the hotel bedroom all weekend with Sam, played games with him, ate meat pies and children's gob-stoppers cheaply out of paper bags and gorged on the all-in breakfast. It came to the third night. The child slept. Albert looked at his watch by the light of the empty television screen. Programmes were long over, but the white screen with the volume down served not badly as a night light; any of the lamps in the shoebox room kept Sam awake, and total darkness made him frightened. Me too, thought Albert; me too. It was three in the morning. What happened tomorrow? Solicitor? School? Work? He must telephone Bella, obviously. Fear of everything ahead burned into him like acid. He wanted never to leave the room. In three days, the gimcrack furniture had become familiar and the two of them had developed habits of eating and passing time that was consoling, like the lives of spies in a loft.

Fear that the next move will be worse. Even the most dismal and unstable circumstances can become something to be clung to. About three o'clock, he telephoned his wife. His best friend answered, in a voice clotted with sleep. Albert panicked, and put the receiver down, which made the next attempt more difficult. It took him an hour. Again he got Jim.

"Tell Bella that Sam's all right," he said to his old friend, in the old friendly tone, because there was no other to be found. "I mean, I'll take him to school tomorrow."

"Where are you, old man?" Jim spoke as if he were telephoning from a golf club instead of a cuckold's bed.

"I'm not saying," said Albert.

Then Bella must have taken the receiver. "You realize what you're doing," she said. "Technically it's kidnapping." She laughed drowsily.

"You're the guilty party," he said, and cursed himself. He did something bold, then talked like a ninny.

"Dear Albert. Really." She laughed again. He longed shamingly for her all the same. "The mother always gets custody." There was a pause. "Where are you?" she said.

"I'm not saying." Even with the volume as low as possible, the closed-down TV still emitted a faint shriek. "You're not going to get Sam," he said. "I've lost enough. It's not as if you really mind. You never wanted him in the first place." He waited, urgently needing news of her. "Are you all right?" he said.

"I'll pick him up from school, then," she said.

"If you do, I'll go to a solicitor."

"Don't be daft, Albert. You bring him back tomorrow or I'll get on to the police."

"I can't talk to you while Jim's there." Couldn't she go downstairs to the other telephone? He realized she must have nothing on. She would have to find a dressing-gown. He felt sick with lust and grief, and had no tongue for any of it.

"You're talking as if I asked you to telephone," she said. "Waking me up. I knew Sam was all right. It's so hysterical. You should know better. You of all people. What about your famous regular life? You were always the one that was on about a regular life."

"I've taken a stand."

She snorted.

"I've come to a decision," he said. Didn't she see it?

The child thrashed and bawled something cheerful in its sleep and lay still again.

"I could have you up, you know," she said lightly, with an adopted benignity that froze him beyond death.

"It's your casualness that gives you away," he said. "I mean, that gives away your guilt." He wasn't a customs officer for nothing. It was his profession that had brought him that shaft of insight, and he felt mildly safer because of it. Another part of him—not a customs officer—told him that guilty people were dangerous, and he wondered in panic what she would do.

"Oh, honestly, Albert. Trotting that out. Giving me your wretched customs clichés at a time like this." Did she mean at four in the morning, or at a time of extremity? The first, probably, in this offhand mood.

"You're not to go near Sam tomorrow, do you hear?" he said.

"Producing self-righteous customs definitions about your own wife. As if I were some Arab with five gold watches up his arm."

"You're not my wife any longer." What had he come out with? The unfaced truth, no doubt. He had the impression that his appendix scar was tearing open, and looked down at it.

"For heaven's sake, let's all get to sleep," she said. "And you'll go back to work tomorrow, because you'd never skip work, would you, Mister Reliable? No matter how much of a crisis. And Sam'll go to school, and you'll pick him up again if you insist on it, and just see how you like it. You won't be able to keep it up for more than a week."

He put the phone down with the usual feeling of life at present, that he could strike forward forever and only land up farther behind. He sought resolve and found a little and went to lie down on the bed to read a paperback of *Anna Karenina*, which he had always fancied because it had a scene on a railway platform. He liked train journeys very much.

"Happy families are all alike; every unhappy family is unhappy in its own way," he read, and his stomach lurched. After the opening page, he noticed that he had retained nothing of what followed and that he was eating a potato crisp. I didn't come over here to eat potato crisps, he thought, and turned over, and cried for Bella, and ate another potato crisp. There's something morbid about my appetite, he thought. Then he made an effort in another direction and tried to rehearse the future—not Monday but the future that lay farther ahead. It struck him suddenly, like the teeth of a trap round his skull, that it was quite possible that he and Bella might never live with each other again. He took in that fact for the first time; in spite of his knowing job, he had a clownish naïveté about fate and always tended to be innocent of the possibility of calamity. He lived by temperament in the eternal present of circuses and drunks. The mortal faculty of looking ahead was granted to him rarely, and then usually at dead of night.

He would see Bella sometimes, he supposed. He would hear news of her, which he would find hard to bear, because a fragment of information about a familiar who has suddenly become perplexing is so insufficient as to be nearly intolerable. What she would feel on hearing news of him he had no idea. Nothing, probably. Perhaps a twinge of malice or discontent, or some dull glee. He felt he knew very little about her present feelings, which were so malign toward him and unmapped that it was as if he were seeing the back side of the moon. Now she told him that he had never understood her in any case. Once she had seemed to know a good deal about him, but in her idle rancour of the last few weeks she had abused him for faults that seemed nothing to do with the truth of him.

If they should meet when the trouble was over, he thought, avoiding the word "divorce" even in his head, they would communicate with difficulty and unease. There were no topics left. It would be impossible for him to speak of their past, or of her, without seeming vulgarly proprietary; or of Jim, without seeming barbed; or of Sam; or even of work. His job had turned into such a jest over the last few weeks that the thought of putting on his uniform, that humiliatingly naval-looking, obviously non-sea-going uniform, made him stiff with bashfulness. She would go on living in their small house, he supposed, and cooking rather well, and hiding small amounts of money touchingly in drawers and atlases. He would go on sleeping badly, and opening people's luggage, and given great luck he would even keep on living with Sam, though it was difficult to imagine that she would seriously consent to give up such a trophy, however little genuine pleasure she had from the child. She would continue to define her ex-husband as diminishingly efficient, and he would go on seeing himself as an ill-equipped buffoon who had stumbled into six years of brazen luck. He would go on thinking of her as a beautiful, hidden woman, with a striking flair for life lying in sulky disuse. And she would take herself for what? He wasn't sure. An ill-served victim, probably, for she had an impregnable trick of seeming the passive one in situations she had generated. He imagined she would always picture herself as a woman too lazy ever to be guilty, with a certain black dash in the late afternoon, and a temperament born two gins below par. And in the meantime he would go on missing her unremittingly, and finding reminders of her everywhere. It seemed unlikely that there would be an end to that. Perhaps she would think of him one day with less ill-will than now, but not for very long at a time; not obsessively, not like this. He longed for a drink, and ate the crust of a sandwich.

They would perhaps build an occasional Bailey bridge between one another because of Sam. Would she marry Jim? Presumably. Or perhaps not, if she retained enough satisfaction in keeping her boring husband on the hook. When they met, they might even have the decency to paper the cracks. In time, perhaps, she would make efforts to conceal her resentment about his ability to make her feel guilty, and he would make efforts to conceal his anguish about the loss of her. It was a dour and racking prospect. For he was going to be burdened always with the conviction that it could have been avoided. He wondered if she would ever regret it, and thought not. Regret was not in her compass. He suddenly remembered writing cheery lewd limericks with her on a train to Yugoslavia, and worrying about the possibility of her getting pregnant there with the child he longed for, bothering about the bad doctors and the heat. Oh my dear, he thought. How terrible, what has happened: I don't know how to deal with any of it.

At seven o'clock he dialled room service, but it was too early. At seven-thirty he dialled again, and could wait no longer to wake Sam. They had a very large breakfast together. Sam was gratified to be alone with his father and identified only the improvization and daring that lay in the situation, not the guilt and apprehension. The small boy ate ten griddle cakes and the man eight. They called for more maple syrup and more butter. A complicity indistinguishable from lovers' happiness ran through the two of them, not localized but suffused through their frames, like alcohol after exercise.

He took Sam to school each day and the airport was accommodating about his hours. He said that his wife was ill. Though he despised the dinginess of the impulse, he transferred half the money in their joint bank account into one of his own at another branch. The airport hotel was an expensive way to live, but they gave him a trade reduction, which seemed the logically absurd extension of a farcical situation. It was ludicrous: a customs officer living with a contraband child, spending half the day in a posture of specious confidence with one foot up on his inspection counter while he intimidated law-abiding passengers, and the other half knowing furtiveness and joy in smuggling around a small boy who was his own and licit son.

He took to having a daily early-morning nip from a half-bottle of whisky in his hip pocket. In the dark hours after breakfast it was some way of controlling the monstrous disjuncture between his private and his public life. He had a sense of subterfuge that was often nearly paralysing. Added to the simple foundation for it, there was the more complex one that he somehow found it essential to hide his wound about Bella from notice. His secrecy about his unhappiness made everything about daily life seem a little counterfeit, apart from meals with Sam and sprees with him at the pictures. The perplexing thing was that Bella, whom he had now nerved himself to telephone every other evening with news of Sam, seemed not to mind the untenable situation particularly and had taken up the flute. The *flute*.

"Are you going to a solicitor?" she said in the end, cushioning her voice as if she didn't care.

"Not unless you try to take Sam away."

That was the balance of power. Both had a mortal deterrent. Bella didn't want to be called guilty; her instinct was always for ambiguity. Albert equally dreaded the law, for though it would find him the injured one, no court would approve of leaving a five-year-old to the care of its father in an airport hotel.

Change had to come. It was something apparently irrelevant that had enough secret bearing on Albert's situation to push him into action. The catalyst was the atmosphere of the airport. Over two or three days it suddenly became malign enough to seem a reflection of Bella's casual slaughter of their lives, and at last he rose in revolt.

The passengers who use an airport will think it too barren of temperament to have anything so interesting as an atmosphere, but for the people who work there its moods are as mutable and contagious as any other place's. During a strike, for instance, there is an anger with stalemate that nothing soothes. In fog there is an atmosphere first of temper and then of inertia, followed by improvization and a peculiarly relieved conviviality, like the illogical sense of reprieve that lies in having to eat a carefully planned picnic lunch inside a car because it is pouring with rain outside.

Soon after Albert had left Bella, London Airport was gripped by the mood of a vicious incident at Immigration. An eighteen-year-old boy who had flown from India to marry a Calcutta girl now living in Liverpool was detained for three days by the officials, who suspected him of being under age and of using marriage as a trick to get a work permit. His desperate girl, ox-eyed, perhaps twelve years old or perhaps thirty-five, waited outside the Customs Hall for him without leaving even to sleep, watching through the glass and crying softly and putting the damp balls of face tissue into a big plastic handbag that looked ugly and moving against her sari. After long-drawn-out bickering, the boy was taken away for a medical examination.

The officials' mood was self-protective and unpleasant. The newspaper reporters who came on to the scene contributed to the overspill of spite. Albert was affected by it and frightened. And then, early one morning, when the affair was still unsettled and he could see the Indian girl asleep on a sofa with one arm through the strap of her handbag and the sari drawn over it, a delayed flight from Jamaica arrived with twelve unaccompanied West Indian children on board. They came down the stairs into customs in procession, wearing party dresses and dull cardigans and silver shoes, with ribbons in their pigtails and a purple tinge under their skin from the cold. Two of them were wearing navy-blue men's overcoats that must have been the crew's, holding the ends carefully to save them from trailing on the stairs. The English porters, who are generally friendly, helped them to find their luggage: brown paper parcels and cardboard boxes and suitcases tied together with string. Albert was joking with the kids and grinning when he heard one of the porters talking, leaning on his luggage-trolley and speaking loudly.

"Send them back where they came from," the porter said to no one in particular, following it with an obscenity. The malevolence was so startling that Albert shook his head as though he had a wasp in his ear. "They're after our jobs." What did the man mean? Ten-year-olds after jobs? "Bread out of our mouths. They've got their own country, haven't they? Who's going to look after them when they fall flat on their face and come whining, that's what I want to know? *Us*, that's who. Bleeding *you-ess*. Off our insurance it'll come. Free dentists, free operations, free tonsils, free milk. It'll be free housing and overtime before you can turn round." He found another porter to address himself to. "You want to put a bit of boot polish on your face, mate. If you're a nig-nog you've got it dead lucky."

Albert had started talking as loudly as possible to the children. They seemed too exhausted to take much in, apart from one little girl who understood very well. Suddenly he exploded, yelled at the porter to buzz off, and broke union regulations by pushing the children's luggage himself to the two West Indian women who were meeting them. One was carrying a string bag with three cauliflowers in it and the other some distressingly expensive-looking toys. Next day he took a week's holiday and went with Sam to Switzerland, because he thought he would enjoy the tobogganing.

They went by train. Making an effort, Albert told Bella where they were going, and she sent a pair of children's ski mitts ahead of them to the pension. Aha, Albert thought— spying on me; and then sat on himself for thinking anything so paranoid. There was no note in the package; only Bella's name and address printed on the customs declaration form. She might have written something to me, he thought. Sending off a pair of mitts, indeed. As if I'd have let Sam's hands freeze. Silky of her. It even looked a bit like Jim's handwriting. Couldn't she be troubled to print the name of her own husband (no, ex-husband) and her own child? Obviously old Jim was trying to muscle in on Sam. "Here," Albert said to himself, "I didn't come all this bleeding way to have Sam's future step-father on my back."

The child slept, sated with the *wagon-restaurant* food, and Albert mooched about the room and fought with the bed-sized pillow that the Swiss take to be practical as an eiderdown. By gum, the address didn't even call him "Esquire". Just "Albert Cruikshank." It was pretty studied of her. (Or of Jim.) Not that he was a stickler for such things; he thought courtesy titles rather silly, in fact; but she always *used* to call him "Esquire". He hurled himself over in bed to study the writing under the lamp, still couldn't decide whether it was Jim's or Bella's, ate a piece of milk chocolate, and then six Codeines, because he had forgotten to bring his sleeping pills. After he had taken them, it occurred to him that the aspirin was possibly a stimulant, not a sedative, and he read the details on the bottle morosely for ten or fifteen minutes, thinking now and then of emetics and vomitoriums and wondering how the Romans did it. The only ingredient he recognized on the prescription was caffeine. That was a stimulant, all right. He must have had the equivalent of a good twelve cups of black coffee. He wouldn't sleep a wink. Damn her, he thought, and pined for her. Bella could always sleep. Coffee knocked her out like a blow on the head. So did a row. Whereas rows kept him awake all night, like lobster. What a thing to do: to send a pair of ski mitts for Sam and nothing for him. It wasn't exactly that he wanted a present. But he was the adult involved, after all, he thought, eating a piece of chocolate hard on a particular tooth to get rid of some bitter aspirin lodged in a broken stopping. Adults suffered more. People made such a fuss about the children of separated parents. What about the separated parent? Sam showed no sign of missing Bella. Unless he was hiding it, of course. Like himself. There was that possibility to be considered. Probably to be considered all *night*, he thought bitterly, dropping off to sleep in his clothes.

Sam and he learned to ski. Sam did it much faster and much better. Albert asked him once if he didn't find it agonizingly painful on the calves, especially in the case of an attempt to stop, but the child obviously didn't know what his father was talking about. The effort of giving Sam as much exercise as he wanted made Albert more fit than he had been for years. Good health gripped him exhaustingly. He slept almost as long as Sam, because there was nothing much else to do but read, and reading put him to sleep anyway. He had intended to learn French and had brought with him a set of books asserting that you could teach yourself French in two weeks, but he didn't open them. He had also brought a chess manual, because he had heard that children could play chess brilliantly, but after ski-ing with Sam for a few days he decided that there was no call to be beaten by a five-year-old at two things at once. *The Red and the Black*, a crossword-puzzle book, and *How to Train Your Labrador*—he had toyed for years with the idea of owning a Labrador—also sat about on the dressing-table and the floor unread. Dropped projects littered the room like old socks.

"Dad," said Sam, drumming him awake with blows on the face, "it's our last day and you're *asleep*."

"What time is it?"

"I don't know. Late."

Albert looked at his watch and found it was only six, but thought it gratuitous to say so. Sam dangled a pair of ski boots in his face. Albert had gone to sleep in his clothes, as usual. He put the boots on in bed.

"I can't understand why you're not stiff," he said. "What do you want for breakfast?"

"Chocolate. No, coffee."

"Chocolate's better for you. Do you really like coffee or are you pretending?"

"I like it with a slug in it."

"What did you say?"

"Like you."

"Listen, that's not for people of five. Anyway, I only have it with a slug in it in the morning."

"Poor old dad." Sam bounced on his face commiseratingly. "How old are you?"

Albert was offended, and swung his legs athletically out of bed, wincing on the distant side of his face. "I'm not really stiff at all," he said, putting his ski boot into a plate of gelantine that he had had in bed for dinner last night.

"Look out," Sam said.

"Why?" said Albert, knocking over a toothglass of Kirsch with his other boot as he tried to scrape the gelantine off the left heel with his right toe.

When they got back the airport hotel seemed like home but his money was running out. Albert started reading *The*

Weekly Advertiser for cheap furnished rooms. He had two days' respite before Bella delivered her deathblows. A solicitor wrote him a letter at the airport, with a copy to the customs authorities, saying that Bella had evidence he was drinking and unfit to have the care of the child, whom he had anyway abducted without written consent. He was sacked at once. An arm of the law arrived the same day to take Sam away from him, and also demanded to see what the man called "the place of lodging". Seen through those jaded, cautious eyes, the messy hotel room seemed something to be protected.

Albert himself took Sam back to Bella. "You're out of your mind. Saying I drink!" he yelled at her.

"Don't shout in front of Sam."

"Don't be pious."

"You've admitted it yourself."

"You've gone mad. You're out of your vicious skull."

"Jim was a witness."

"You've made up every word of it and you know it. Where *is* Jim?"

"At work, of course. He's made an affidavit about what you said."

The multiplying sins took his breath away. He could find nothing to say. "I have an opinion, that's all!" he shouted finally.

"You're bluffing," she said. "You've nothing to say."

How could she always appear to be so right? Even to him? Perhaps she *was* right.

He went away and got a job as a waiter in a bad restaurant in Soho. It suited his mood. Bella's slander about drink baffled him, but at the same time it queerly took root, until he did indeed start boozing a good deal. He was in the restaurant kitchen late one night before closing up, knocking back the remains of four glasses of liqueur from a dirty table, when his head suddenly cleared and he heard some lines from the past in a devastating playback in his head: "You're better off without me"—Bella's voice, coolly justifying herself to him on the telephone. "A bachelor's life suits you far better. You never liked living with me, anyway."

"It's simply not true. We were happy. How can you have forgotten? I can't bear living on my own."

"You're not on your own. You've got Sam, who you say means so much to you. You're deceiving yourself about that too, of course."

"I can hardly cope without you."

"You're functioning beautifully. Mister Reliable."

"I tell you I can hardly manage. I have to have a drink every morning straight after breakfast to get through. What do you think it's like? You with Jim. Both of you lost."

He had thought they were at least speaking to one another privately, but if Jim had really sworn an affidavit he must have been listening on another telephone. So even that small intimacy with her was a deceit. Or his own self-deception; she had unseated him too deeply for him to be sure any longer of the distinction. He found some more dregs of many different drinks and tossed them down. A young couple came to the door of the restaurant, which said "Closed", and made pleading gestures to be let in. He crouched down behind the service hatch in an instinct not to be seen, and then the alcohol stirred in his veins and he was emboldened to be rebuking, lecturing them about making a noise and then, with extreme lordliness, cooking them a very bad meal at no charge. He did it not because he liked people that night but to make a moral point about something or other. He was obviously in the right. Or *had* been in the right. Though Bella had now eerily made him wrong. But he was bound to be right still about something. Such as stealing a couple of meals from his boss, for instance, he thought, shaking Worcester sauce merrily onto two steaks to cover the taste of burning.

Bella asked for a divorce because she was going to marry Jim. She said, through her solicitor, that she wanted no maintenance for Sam. She was getting a job. Bella a *job*? When Albert missed the child most urgently, the refusal of money for him seemed like a moral tactic to take him away forever. But no, Bella said through her solicitor; to see the child, Albert had only to ring up. Which he couldn't do now for all the tea in China. He took himself to the call-box in his lodgings night after night, but whether he was sloshed or sober there was no way of finding the nerve to dial. He went without a sight of any of them for a year.

Once he read something in a paper about Bella; she seemed to have done rather well. It said she was a fashion adviser in "a famous West End store". There was a picture of her in something described as "at-home trousers". Albert cut it out, snipping around the paragraph that said that her husband was the buyer in the men's sports-clothes department of the same store, and pinned up the clipping in his room. Jim a *sports-clothes* buyer. Then he took the clipping down again because the photograph made her look thin. Or perhaps she actually was thin now. Thinned by Jim, by

Jove, by gum. He had another drink. He had always liked her better fat himself.

One day he saw them both through the window of a hotel bar when he was sitting on a bus in Shaftesbury Avenue. The bus was in a traffic jam right opposite them. They seemed to be having a quarrel. Not a bad one, perhaps. After gesticulating at each other, they both fell silent and looked at their drinks. Bella was indeed thinner and looked distantly smart. Then the bus moved on again into his own particular vacuum. He missed even the sight of them acutely. He had been sacked last week, for the fourth time in a year, after a row with an unpleasant restaurant owner who had a fat pink face that looked about to snort, and chaste little feet on raised heels that he walked on as if they were trotters. The row had been about drinking; it generally was. Or rather, about finishing up customers' drinks, for when Albert came in on a Monday morning drunk at his own expense none of his morally outraged proprietors had ever turned a hair. Hypocrites! he thought, and entertained a fugitive idea that Bella and Jim needed him.

Later that evening—many glasses later, and four or five hours—he took a bus to his old house and lurched gaily along the interminable suburban road. He was wearing a duffel coat, done up on the wrong toggles, with copies of evening papers turned back at the job columns sticking out of both pockets. His hair, which he had cut himself in one of the gales of thrift that blew up in him every few weeks, kept getting into his eyes and caused him to see a charming rainbow when he stood under a street lamp to look up at Sam's room—something he had done too often. Enough of loitering, he said to himself. I'll be turning into a voyeur next. The drainpipe needed mending. Old Jim had looked a bit got down, he thought; I'll cheer them up, and we'll all have a drink. Quite a gesture, turning up at this hour. They'd be more nervous than he was. He'd have to put them at their ease. He yelled abuse at a dog that was about to turn up the garden path, doing it more for form's sake than because he disliked dogs, and then Jim opened the door and unfortunately called the animal inside.

"Hallo, old man," Albert said, realizing that his face was invisible against the light of the street lamp. "It's me."

"Who's me?"

It was a bad foot to start on. However, Albert got over that, and so did Jim, and they went into the sitting-room, where Bella was sitting in mini-gear frighteningly too young for her, with office folders on her lap.

"Working late?" said Albert chattily.

They talked about the store where Bella and Jim worked. Jim sat down by the fire in Albert's old chair and then reversed direction and got up again in one amazing movement. He stood in front of the fire instead and said, "Sit down, old man."

Albert said that the work sounded very interesting, concentrating on getting vim and colour into his voice. Jim said that the store had a first-rate food department and a bank. Albert said joyfully that he must start using it, then. The mention of a bank made him feel guilty about not having a joint account with Bella any longer. His self-reproaches had been in pickle for a year, and the notion that they might be out-of-date escaped him. He found it impossible to keep in his head for any length of time that Bella wasn't still his wife. "You don't mind not having a joint account, do you, darling?" he said to her. "I mean, it seemed sensible."

"We've *got* one," said Jim. "What do you mean?"

Bother him. Other times, other spouses, thought Albert, and the floor rocked. He kept an eye on it. He noticed that Jim was wearing some very expensive-looking clothes, and feared he might be spending all Bella's earnings on his own back.

"I hope you get a discount," Albert said. "On clothes."

"Bella gets a lot of hers free," said Jim. "The manufacturers let her have things, you know. And trips to Paris. . . ."

"Sam's going to a new school," Bella said, and time was oddly foreshortened in Albert's head so that two or three minutes of silence passed between them and he thought it only a second.

"We're going to take him to Italy when I go over for the collections. We thought the trip would be nice for him," Bella said. Then she remembered that she was supposed to get the father's permission before taking the child out of the country, and said, "If you agree, that is." She looked away from the tramp in her drawing-room to Jim in his Italian shirt and black doeskin trousers.

Albert said graciously, "I'd be delighted for Sam to have a holiday with you. With both of you." The floor appeared to be attacking his face. He shook his head quickly as if he were warding off a sneeze and concentrated on Jim, whose affable plasticine face now seemed sharper and more ambitious. He and Bella didn't seem to be having very much fun without him. Not up to the old days; not for either of them. "Let's have some champagne," said Albert. "I'll treat you."

"There's nowhere open, and we haven't got any, have we, dearest?"

"There's a bottle under the stairs," said Albert. "I put it there myself for an emergency like this. I mean an occasion like this."

"It'll be warm," Jim said.

"I'll ice the glasses," said Albert.

It occurred to him as he was crashing about in the cupboard among his own old mackintoshes, tennis racquets, gum boots, and broken picture frames that he might be doing the wrong thing.

"You don't mind my using the house as if it were my own?" he cried with as much boisterousness as he could muster, waving the bottle like a flag. Bella lit a cigarette, which she smoked now with a holder. She looked frosty, so Albert tried a friendly guffaw. "I'll go and get the ice," he said, pushing on with it.

Jim sprang up, but Bella raised her eyebrows at him and said, "It's no use."

The fridge was full of delicious things and Albert tried a few of them. Then he started making a plate for them all. Again time must have passed very quickly, for Jim came out to look for him.

"Hello," Albert said, with his mouth full of paté. "Just getting us all a little something."

"Have you got a job?" Jim said, sitting on a plastic stool and looking like a husband in an ideal kitchen advertisement. Albert suddenly thought with loyalty of cockroaches and other vermin.

"I've given it up for the moment," he said.

"What were you doing?"

"Waiter." He sucked a thumb with some gravy under the nail from a pie that he had investigated. "Bella's a good cook, isn't she?" he said. "You've put on weight, old boy."

This cut Jim, because it was true; the new Italian doe-skin trousers were a size bigger than his usual.

"It suits you," Albert said kindly, seeing his face. "Honestly."

"Wouldn't you like to take your duffel coat off?" said Jim, seeing that there was a cuff in the butter.

The atmosphere when they opened the bottle seemed to Albert to improve no end. Bella and Jim needed some gaiety. Dull dogs now, he thought. I must buck them up. He tried a few jokes to breach their blandness. It wasn't easy. What a pair, he thought, as joke after joke hit fog. Nevertheless, at whatever cost, he must perk things up. After all, that was what he had come for. The night wore on; time alternately pelted and ground to a stop. Albert fell prey to his nightly fantasies of living with Bella again and began looking at Jim with rage in his heart toward the wet blanket who was preventing it. Yet he couldn't quite drum up the enmity that seemed necessary in the circumstances, and that fact quite pleased him, for it proved what an enduring thing male friendship was, even if Jim did look to him less than his old self, and over-dressed in foreigners' plumes that must have cost a packet in duty, the jacket obviously being pure wool. The levy due on hundred-per-cent woollen goods made him remember other customs regulations, and then instantly of his contraband Sam.

"Can I see him?" he said, gesturing upward with his head to Sam's bedroom.

"He's away," Bella said.

Albert eyed her carefully, correcting a possible squint in his gaze, and decided she was lying. "I can hear him breathing," he said irritably.

"Jim, can we get him home?" Bella said.

"Have some black coffee, old man," Jim said.

Bella telephoned for a taxi.

"I can hear him *breathing*," said Albert again, making for the door to the stairs. Jim tried coaxing him away with a glass of brandy, which Albert thought a low device. He could indeed hear breathing, though it was true of course that it might be his own, since everything about himself seemed to be happening so far away for the moment.

"I'm not having a drunk near my child," Bella said. "Jim, see if you've got any clothes we could give him."

"I'm not a drunk. I just drink," said Albert.

"I don't know how you afford it. Jim says you're out of work. Do you want a job?"

Jim came back with some clothes over his arms and stood at the door, while Bella very slowly told Albert to come and be interviewed next week for a job as a public-relations officer in their department store. She said she would fix it, as long as he stayed off the drink.

"You're spoiling the party," Albert said desperately. "You and Jim want jollying up a bit." He told them another long joke and won a laugh out of Bella that sealed the success of the evening for him. Jim stayed at the door with the clothes over his forearm, listening and waiting. He looked servile, Albert said happily to himself—not like a man of command passing on old clothes at all; more like a foot-man waiting for an end of his master's good-byes.

"Is Sam really away?" he said.

"You can see him if you keep this job," Bella said.

He went up for the job, grinding his teeth, and got it. He gave Jim's clothes away to a refugee organization and pawned his watch to buy some clothes of his own choice for the interview. He did the craven work for two months, see-ing Sam every weekend, until it came to a meeting at which he was supposed to speak: a report about a provincial store promotion scheme. The meeting was called for a Monday, at three o'clock in the afternoon. He spent the weekend without a single drink, for Sam's sake, as he saw it. And then on Monday morning things moved around in his head and he started drinking quite a lot, also for Sam's sake, to toast the victory of seeing him once more and to say a damn to caution. By the time he arrived at the meeting, the floor was slanting like a deck again. He had bought a bunch of parsley on his way in, because he had heard that it clears away the smell of alcohol. He ate the bunch in the staff lift in front of two girl assistants, joking nervously and making rabbit faces at them. They thought him quite mad.

The boardroom was full of women in hats and men in dark suits who looked like a convention of dentists. Albert realized that he had forgotten his report, but trusted his memory to make it up. To his pleasure, he saw Bella there. Bella would get him through.

The talk of promotion schemes and window displays was hard to listen to. The stocking buyer's nose began to fascin-ate him. It was long and pointed, like a quill, and she wore a hat that seemed to have a beak. The faces along the table started to look like the masks of animals in a zoo and struck him as needing his help to get out. When it came to his turn to speak, he took his time, lit a thin Italian cigar, and leaned back in his chair to think about them.

"Mr Cruikshank," said the chairman, a woman all in brown from Balenciaga. "The report."

He started to speak. He suddenly felt horribly drunk, but his wits had not altogether left him and he had a nasty inkling that his speech was not to the point. He seemed to be split into three clear elements, all of them aching with good intent and a longing to sound some clarion call not to hold back. For the first part, there was his voice, managing quite efficiently without him. For the second, there was a sense of desperate fortitude and a desire to conquer obstacles not yet quite in sight. For the third, there was the pang in his body, physical, yet presumably more to do with the mind: a regret for the paltriness of his life; grief about an existence that seemed in perpetual stalemate now because of a devouring sense of loss and betrayal, and yet a certainty of the possibility of something else. All at once he wanted to win them over, the people in the boardroom, win them with his candour and his vision of a better country. At the same time he was aware that he was growing hard to understand and that he must have fallen into spitting, because the corset buyer opposite was glaring at him and wiping her face with a lace handkerchief.

"Leeds, Mr Cruikshank. The Young-As-You-Feel promotion in Leeds," said a voice. The voice spread like ink through blotting paper and seeped across his mind until it reached the nerve that knew it to be Bella's.

"Ladies and Gentlemen—Madam Chairman, I should say, ladies and gentlemen, my wife, my ex-wife.... As I say, Leeds is a city ready ... ready for hipster tights.... A toast! As I was saying, it's a god-awful hole. But the fact is there is something happening.... As I said, England.... As I said, Madam Chairman. Yes!" He took a long puff on his beautiful cigar and tapped the ash into a wastepaper basket full of mimeographed reports. "My wife, England, is experiencing, in my profound conviction, a renewal. She might seem to you to be a vulgar woman, cautious, opportunist—I don't know how she seems—but there is something ready to...." He heard his voice shouting and lowered it carefully. The people around the table watched the papers in the basket smoulder and begin to smoke. "One must pay attention," Albert said. "We must all pay more attention. To notice.... Notice more, yes, about the way we live.... Bella had a better life once, I swear it.... But I didn't attend.... God help.... Perfidy and ambition and swinging gear. It's a bad time I tell you. A bad ... England.... You don't listen. I shall enjoy my cigar."

The corset buyer got to her feet grimly and picked up the glass of drinking water in front of her. Before she could throw the water into the wastepaper basket, the reports had gone up in smoke. Albert seemed to notice last, and his face expressed less than anybody's. Then he rather undercut the room's prim pity for him by roaring with laughter.

Known for her Frankness

"What *are* dialectics?" said Anthony, looking for his agent's kit-bag and make-up case on the baggage trolley at Frankfurt Airport and speaking with as much truculence as he could ever muster.

Maud tapped her cigar and said, "You mean what *is* dialectics. I predict that the car will crash. Then I drive it at a brick wall. The car crashes. I am right."

"Ah."

"Though properly understood, dialectics is the muscle of the drama."

Anthony still wondered if it shouldn't be "are the muscle". No: "The wages of sin *is* death." But no one would actually ever say such a thing. Though that wasn't entirely true, for Maud would, and she would probably even bring it off. To have the character to give sanction to grammar—phew! Maud talked with a mixture of pedantry and horse sense that impressed him as singular and forcible. Sometimes he tried to catch her style in scraps of speech that he wrote in a notebook, because she had often told him to listen to the way strangers talked and to keep a record of conversations overheard in the Underground. But for reasons that he took to be his own error in transcription, anything that he pilfered straight from life never sounded convincing. She could make him doubt most things about himself, but not the accuracy of his ears. He might put down until kingdom come the dully literal truth of the way she talked, but when it was written out it was clearly not credible, except maybe as the English of Nkrumah, or of an Eskimo who had studied the language by gramophone record.

Her style on paper, in her manuals about how to write, was rather different. It was terse and practical, a little like a dog trainer's. In the quiet of his own skull he called it manly, but he would never have used such a word to her, not only because she was privately decorous but also because the way she talked about her children made him sense that she dreaded being thought lesbian. The blight she cast on his work was something he didn't care to inspect, for she certainly wished him well. Before she had taken him over he must have written too easily. Then he read a textbook of hers about the craft of the dramatist and it had stopped him from showing her anything for a year. There was a chapter in it titled "So You Think You're Chekhov". The very thought had crossed his mind only the day before, when he contemplated giving up doctoring, as she kept telling him to. He felt appalled at her insight, and at his own cheek. There was another chapter called "Study Your Market, Not Your Navel".

"I'd like something to drink," she said while he was putting the luggage together.

He spoke to the porters in English, because he was trying to forget that he had spent the first ten years of his life in Berlin.

"Practise your German," she said.

In the airport restaurant he asked her what she would like.

"A plain soda water. With ice."

"It seems to be all beer," he said after reading the menu for a long time. "They don't give you any alternatives. How German."

"*An* alternative. They don't seem to give you *an* alternative. There can never be more than one alternative. *Alter, alter*—one of two."

"Aren't you feeling well? No, I didn't mean—I meant about wanting soda water?"

"Aeroplane food is inspissating. My tongue feels like a rug. We ate better in Hall at Oxford." The days of reading philosophy, politics, and economics, called PPE, came up a good deal. "I've just sold a comedy of Philip's about air travel," she said. "It's ill-executed, I'm afraid. My fault. It was my topic. I gave it away to the wrong person. No, I correct myself: for the wrong reason. I'd hoped to get the poor man writing again. But he's sold out. My God, he's sold out. Still, I suppose the play's commercially viable. Everyone abominates air travel, though they all do it. What a travesty of Mary Wortley Montagu." She ran a comb through her cropped hair.

"It's awfully good of you to have come with me," he said, feeling he should apologize for something, and kicking as powerfully as possible against the fancy that he was Philip.

"It's a poor play. I hate it, frankly." ·

He remembered a girl he had known once who used to say "*franchement*" whenever she meant "frankly"—rather a soupy girl, and far from frank, but consoling all the same

on despairing Sundays, and she had made beautiful cas-
seroles.

"Philip hasn't written a real play for four years," Maud
said, looking round for the waiter. "I've told him so perfectly frankly. He's funking it."

"I must get you your soda water."

"It looks to me as if there's some system of getting service
that you don't grasp."

"No, I don't think so. Really? Oh." He floundered, and
then clicked his fingers, doing it hesitantly, because it
seemed like the worst of the British raj in India. But no one
can click his fingers hesitantly.

"Why don't you shout something to him?"

"I hadn't realized how much I was going to hate speaking
German again."

She snorted. "You mustn't funk it. Once you get over it,
there's your play."

"Two soda waters with ice, please," he said eventually to
a waiter who looked like Himmler.

"It is absolutely forbidden to have soda except with
whisky," Himmler said.

"Two coffees, then," Anthony said in German, trying a
grin to rinse out the sounds in his mouth.

"What's happening?" Maud asked. "Why are you
laughing?"

"He says it is absolutely forbidden to have soda except
with whisky. It's so German, that's all. It's exactly what I
remember." Kindergarten in Berlin in 1936. Special Jewish
kindergarten. His Jewish mother pretending there was
nothing special about it at all, and pouring chicken soup
with barley down his throat.

Maud made a swatting gesture against his amusement. "Why didn't you ask for Perrier water, then?" she said. "They must surely possess Perrier water."

"I wonder if you have Perrier water," Anthony said. "Or Pellegrino?"

"Mineral water," said the waiter. "You have to have."

"Is the mineral water still or sparkling?" Anthony asked, trying to foresee snags. In his consulting room he was good at it.

"Yes," the waiter said.

"What?" Maud said.

"He says mineral water we have to have," Anthony said. "I mean, we have to have mineral water." He laughed again, without looking forward to a thing.

"I hope it's sparkling," Maud said. "Surely mineral water's *bound* to be still. They must have *something* sparkling. *Something* like soda."

"Soda is absolutely forbidden except with whisky," the waiter said. "Because it is permitted only to charge a profit of sixty pfennigs if soda is served with whisky."

Anthony started to translate this, out of an inability to do anything else with it, and when he turned round again the waiter had disappeared. There was a silence of a sort that he knew very well. It seemed especially designed to give weight to his ineptitudes, lending a ridiculous dignity in space to what he had screwed up, like making a free-hanging sculpture of a broken egg-whisk.

Maud salvaged him as usual by noticing nothing, and he mistakenly respected her instinct for dealing with his doldrums. She went on talking strongly, attacking Philip's decline as a playwright, the way he had compromised and run dry by doing translations and hack comedies. And once he had been at *Oxford*, she said. He had got a *Double First*. In *PPE*.

Then the waiter came back, with two glasses of soda. "I have brought you what you absolutely insisted upon having," he said.

"What's he saying now? He's brought the soda perfectly agreeably. You must have misunderstood him. Your German can't be as fluent as you think."

"He did say one couldn't . . ." Anthony said. But the next thing to be said was "Thank you very much" in German, as quickly as possible. No point in behaving like some second German. But he *was* German, of course. Ex-German, rather. Jewish. A Londoner. A doctor. A future playwright. No, a playwright already, by gum. ("So You Think You're Chekhov.") He thought with envy of the young locum doctor standing in for him at home, seeing his patients at this very moment, and then he thought of his ex-wife, and and his ex-cat, which used to sleep on their bed, and then with interest and longing of flukes, the flukes of absorption that can at least put the unforgettable at some merciful remove.

The waiter set down the glasses, saying, "It should be entirely forbidden."

Maud smiled at the man, which struck Anthony as expedient of her, and said to Anthony, "How do I say thank you?"

"I've said it already," Anthony said.

She ignored it. "He's been charming," she said. "I'm afraid you've been churlish. It's understandable, of course, with your history."

They went out through a door that was marked "Hours of Opening: 08.00 to 23.59". Anthony laughed again, at which Maud felt curious while her face stone-walled. It was a habit of disguise that she recognized as costly but could not be rid of. The waiter bawled at them triumphantly and kicked the door with his shoe to point out another notice, which said in English "No Passing".

"No passing," Maud said. "Even I can read that."

"No *passing*!" Anthony laughed again in some torment. "*Everything* brings—brings things back." When words ran as thin on him as this, he sometimes managed to suppose that it meant he was unconsciously saving them to write with. But generally it was plain to him that the cause was his familiar and wringing insufficiency.

"You mustn't get subjective," Maud said. "Don't investigate *your* troubles. People don't want to hear about that. See it *their* way."

He was starting to feel like a bundle of notes about himself in a case-history folder in hospital, one of the folders labelled "NOT TO BE HANDLED BY PATIENT."

In Berlin his past rose to his teeth. Maud had put him into a small hotel near the street where he was born, telling him to absorb the atmosphere. He was supposed to be germinating a television programme for her, on her own topic, about the conscience of an escaped East Berliner. She had told him she was fed up with plays about love—which she spelled out "l-u-v" as if she were saying "b-e-d" to another grown-up in front of a child who might be going to throw a tantrum—and that she wanted to hear about some public issues for a change. Sick with longing for his wife, Diana, and worn out with the public issues of doctoring that had apparently lost her to him, he had agreed.

He tried to think about the Wall. He could see the passion of the theme, but its substance eluded him. He was in the grip of more personal and random emotions. After a few days in his efficient hotel bedroom, the rage and shame of having any connection with West Berlin passed into glassy remorse. He felt more like a hole in the air than ever, and began also to seem frighteningly insensible. He could have stuck pins into himself and it would have taken ten seconds for his body to complain. He slept ten or twelve hours a day and didn't answer Maud when she telephoned. This was the furtiveness that could become fear: not owning up to a language he spoke, smuggling sausages into his bedroom, pretending he was out, plaguing the porters for a letter from his wife when he knew she didn't know where he was. He began to have the spy's terror, the terror caused by one's own silence. He saw Maud once in the Kurfürstendamm, eating alone in a café and looking a little desolate, with a stack of coins already piled beside her plate although her meal had only just come. Instead of keeping her company he dodged into a doorway to watch her. She had ordered no wine. Perhaps her money was running out. In the middle of eating she got up to telephone. He thought her not easily distinguishable from the Berlin women, with their detestable white felt bowler hats, who still looked much as George Grosz had drawn them thirty-five years ago. But there was also something isolated about her, and the battered mannish brief-case against the leg of her chair was touching. She came back from the telephone booth quickly, looking distracted. When he got to the hotel, she had left another message. "Please telephone back urgently any time until 4 a.m."

He felt like a pursued husband, though not like any husband that he had ever been himself. In his own life it had always been he who was the supplicant, telephoning Diana from call boxes on his rounds in the hope of closing some nagging gap of intimacy left at breakfast, and always having to hide the agony of dread that her casualness could cause him for fear of the danger of irritating her. She was never in now when he tried to make contact with her. Nor had she answered messages through friends, and she had written to him only twice in his makeshift London digs—once to say she hoped he was well, and once about some dry cleaning. He couldn't even put together a picture of her day any longer, because she hadn't allowed him to see the Bloomsbury rooms where she lived, though he had mooned by them in his car often enough, at the starts of many nights doomed to reveries of longing and revenge. He spent the black hours best in the writing of hopelessly happy propositions to her that he kept for comfort in a drawer, as if they were love letters received from her instead of dead ones from himself that he saw no good in posting. His memory of her became dulled and blocked, a stalemate of the imagination that began to have the taste of sloth and suicide, like the evil torpor that can ensue from spending night after night without a dream. When he finally had a nightmare about the loss of her, at least it supplied him with a landscape to imagine her in again; there was some spasm of life in that, he supposed.

*

Maud caught him in the doorway of his hotel one evening. "You never ring me back," she said.

"I have tried. You've been out."

"There were never any messages."

"You know what hotels are like."

"I was concerned about you."

"I'm all right."

"I don't like not knowing what you're doing. Are you working?"

The muscles under her eyelids clenched, and the skin on the bone of her forehead moved back like the hood of a snake. Was she angry? Something else.

"I must talk to you," she said. "Otherwise there's no point in my being in Berlin at all."

"I thought you were here for lots of other reasons as well. You said you had to come anyway."

"Are you getting somewhere with the script?"

"I'm doing my puny best."

"Is it coming along?"

He felt precisely as if he were hiding something from her.

"Am I going to be pleased with it?" She pursued him to the porter's desk.

"There's nothing." What on earth had made him say that? He sounded as if he were denying an affair. That was what it felt like. Yet all he was doing was not writing, and missing his lawful wife. He was in the middle of more grief than he could deal with, yet he was piling onto it the commonplace misery of subterfuge, as if he had to protect some clandestine happiness that didn't even exist.

To shake off the mood of secrecy, he took her out. The

balance of power must have shifted between them, because he had a few glittering moments of objectivity about her as well as the old nuzzling gratitude of some broken-kneed dray horse. For once, too, she seemed to want him to order, and to pay the bill.

"Here's to your play," she said when they had decided to have another brandy. "The play of public conscience."

"I don't know about that."

"A reprieve from the telly of l-u-v."

"I feel in more of a muddle about politics every moment."

"Not 'muddle'. At least dignify it as ambiguity."

She was quite handsome in her own brazen key. He had had too much brandy, and he suddenly thought that her face looked like a Buick. To make up for the unkindness, he made a bad and nervous joke. She responded, not laughing but sucking in her cheeks like a man blowing onto his hands in cold weather. He saw himself as a buffoon with nasty reserves of observation, a man with goonish spectacles clamped round his ears and perfidy in his guts, and he felt so appalled by his mistrust of an old friend who must surely be taken for an ally that he tried as fast as possible to invent some headway on the project about Berlin.

"You're lying to me," she said.

"I don't know what you mean." It was like a B feature about a married row.

"You haven't written a line." All he had written, she knew, were letters to his ex-wife in his head; she could smell it. "You're unhappy. You're obsessed with Diana, aren't you?"

"No. Yes. I can't help it, anyway. Why should I?"

"You do extend a prodigious welcome to ghosts."

"Anyway, I have written quite a lot," he lied, in splendid good heart.

"*Really.*"

"Quite a bit. I think it's going to be a comedy."

"You've never written a comedy. It's not a very promising subject for humour." She checked herself. "Well, it's a daring idea. I believe in you, you know." Because she had been aggressive again, she pulled out her wallet and showed him photographs of the children.

He had invented the idea of the comedy at that moment, and to prove it he had to offer her a joke in evidence. "I'm going to put in a few of those brutal German proverbs that don't mean anything. Like 'A hungry belly has no ears'."

She started to say that to her this sounded more like Khrushchev, and she stopped herself again; the line was so clearly a proffering of comfort. He was surely telling her the truth, surely, with that playful-sounding promise of a comedy about the Wall. "You mustn't be unhappy," she said with an edge. Every punishing sense she possessed told her that he was going to write about his wife.

"I do try not to be."

She put on an adopted cosy accent to make him laugh, but she was no mimic and the effort was arthritic. "It's all in the mind."

"I know, but that's where I have to live." He smoked a cigarette and looked at her stubbly hair and bought her another brandy. "I can't think of a toast," he said. "Never mind the blessed television. Here's to—oh, all the other writers you look after. Here's to Philip."

"Have you ever heard of the Slavonic banquet?" she said. "It's a Polish image for the Russian method of killing off the inconvenient. The Russians invite any dangerous questioners to a sumptuous feast, and during the embraces and the toasts the guests are quietly poisoned."

"What do you mean by that? You don't mean that *you're* the guest?"

She made no answer.

"What do I do?" he said later, very drunk.

"There's nothing to do."

Next day, she sent him a huge parcel of books about Germany. She also enclosed a little leather-bound copy of Heine's love poetry, with a jocular luggage label on it that read, "This is *not* what you are writing about!!!" There was a plain white card inside as well, saying, "Only the artist realizes that some of us exert a Homeric effort simply to behave ordinarily," but she had translated her declaration to him into Latin in a self-defeating impulse to disown it, and he never troubled to puzzle it out.

He read some of the German books, soothed by her solicitude and fancying for a time that he really was being impregnated with ideas about the Wall. He felt like a potato in the soil dreaming of the vodka that was to be made of it. Then the endless writing of love letters in his head crashed through the barrier into fiction, and he put his fierce lament for a fled wife onto paper.

Maud waited patiently for him to finish, with only a sliver of dread, and they came back together to London. They did the second half of the journey by train. The compartment was filled by two middle-aged German couples with a sticky and unhappy child. Both couples mysteriously spoke in English, with heavy accents. The jolliness of the return was very unlike the thorny mood of the journey out. Maud was buoyant with complicity, and Anthony robust because he was free of his work.

"Would you like a cup of coffee?" he said to her at a station, and she grinned at him over the cardboard beaker, holding it with both hands.

One of the Germans, wearing a surprising black-and-white checked cloth cap, made an operation out of buying coffee through the window, and held up the train while he got a missing straw. "I took up the cups of coffee, *five* cups, and they give me only *four* straws, not five," he explained carefully. He drew in his breath sharply and gave the change to his wife, who put it into a double-clasped purse, which was then hidden in the inner pocket of a locked hand-bag. He watched the method anxiously.

"Now we got to wash up our fingers and later we eat," said the second man, when he had collected the paper cups and straws.

"We might go and have lunch," Anthony said to Maud, looking at the preparations for eating in the compartment —napkins tucked into shirt collars, laps spread with paper bags. The code of agreement he assumed gave Maud pleasure.

When they came back an hour and a quarter later, the meal seemed scarcely begun.

"I got here tongue as well," the man in the checked cap was saying. "Tongue. I have various packets. These our sister-in-law put in. And the tin of milk. And a plum. And a peach."

"A straw for the tea," said the second man, pouring from a thermos.

"No."

"No?"

"No."

"Sugar."

"I take sugar never either."

"I without milk take it also."

"Have a cigarette," Anthony said to Maud.

"Thank you," Maud said.

"I haven't got anything to read."

"I'm not sure that I could concentrate," she said, as near to humour as he had ever seen her.

He wondered whether to give her his typescript to read. Perhaps she really wouldn't be able to concentrate. Yet he badly wanted her to. He thought it might be good.

"We will real Americans be and with our hands chicken eat," the second man said. He had kept on his hat. It was a brown derby, worn straight on the head without an air. "One half of a gherkin," he said, unwrapping a small thin package in disgust. "What can you do with one half of a gherkin?" He flapped it like a galosh.

"Would you like to read the blessed typescript?" Anthony asked.

"Are you sure?"

"I'd like you to."

He found it an impossible spectacle to watch, and walked up and down the corridor for nearly two hours. He thought it unlikely she would be influenced by the disappointment he had dealt to her plan for a play about the Wall. She was too generous an agent for that.

"Sorry about no Berlin," he said when he finally returned to the compartment.

"You can't be held responsible for your distaste for politics, I suppose." She had her fingers awkwardly in five or six places in the typescript.

"Are those parts that worry you?"

She pulled her fingers out quickly. "Things that struck me."

"Struck you how?"

One of the German men undid yet another thermos and offered Maud some chocolate in a cup, with a straw. She shook her head. The smell in the compartment was nauseating.

"How is the strudel consisted?" one of the women asked.

"Come into the corridor," Maud said. Her dislike and fear of the typescript burned in her head. This couldn't be jealousy, she told herself. No. More like ordinary disappointment, multiplied to a point that was nearly unbearable. "The blow fell with the merciless swiftness of all misfortune"—it was someone else's line, a client's presumably. "My dear boy," she said, lighting a cigar. "I'm probably not fitted to speak about this."

"Why?"

"Knowing your circumstances."

"What?"

"Your Diana."

"It's not autobiographical."

"No. The power of feeling is."

"That makes it sound good."

"Do you want me to speak frankly?"

"Of course."

"I think you shouldn't give up doctoring. I think there's less disappointment in it for you than in writing."

"What are you trying to say? That you think it's awful?"

She was silent.

"You're just peeved that it's not about your subject, that's all. All agents are eunuch writers. I wish you'd just take your ten per cent and leave us alone." He looked round at her, standing beside him in the corridor bar looking out at the stupid countryside. She was crying, for heaven's sake.

"Do you know what it's like?" she said. "You use us as conveniences. We're not just secretaries to fix the Belgian rights."

"That's exactly what you are. You sound like all those parents who complain that their children use the house like a hotel. Of *course* they do. All children do. And so will *their* children. Writers have agents simply to do maths and whoring for them. And to get loot. And perfectly handsomely you do out of it. I don't begrudge your cut. But it doesn't mean I owe you anything, either."

"Except possibly friendship."

"Fine kind of friendship to kick a new piece of work in the teeth."

"We were happy just now. And in Berlin."

"Happy? I'm very fond of you. You've been very good to me. But you're not being honest, not for a moment. We were both miserable in Berlin. I've never felt so lonely in my life. And you were just inventing errands to stay around."

"Because I wanted to."

"Out of benevolence. I missed Diana every moment. I was down a hole. I kept falling asleep at the wrong time like an old tramp. The writing got me through, not you. It was a way of wrangling with my own cowardice, that's all. You can get an edge on yourself by writing. I'm not saying the thing's great, but it's not bad."

"I think it may well be very good. I said I wasn't equipped."

"First you say you're not equipped, then you say go back to doctoring, then you say it may be good. You take a position and then you say things on either side of it. What *is* this frankness of yours?"

"*Each* side. You mean that I say things *each* side of it. Not 'either' side. 'Either' side isn't what you mean."

He looked explosive, and then laughed and gave her a kiss on her flushed and papery cheek and bought them both a bottle of wine in the *wagon* restaurant for tea. He took his typescript with him from the compartment for fear of its vanishing. She told him she didn't want to be his agent any longer if he didn't need her advice, though it would be pleasant if he ever wanted her friendship. She behaved with dignity, in a pain that he perceived without comprehension of it.

In the taxi, while he was dropping her at her small house in Fulham, she made an effort to regain some inch of the indispensable contact she had squandered, but there seemed no way of doing it. The pint of milk and newspapers that she had ordered for her arrival were correctly outside the front door.

"Coming home is as difficult as going away," Anthony said, aware of having behaved kickedly. "Fear of the next step, I suppose."

"Cowardice isn't the worst vice."

"What a curious thing for you to say. When you can't ever have been guilty of it."

She shook her head vehemently, with tears flying out of her eyes each side, like water flying off a spaniel's ears.

He speculated about what she was coming back to. Empty house, chagrin perhaps that he hadn't heeded her theme, loss of face with the TV company, negligent children? An old affair with some woman who had hurt her? The thought did come to his mind a week or so later that she might have been in love with him, but it seemed a ludicrous idea as well as self-congratulatory, and he put it by.

The Redhead

When the skulls in the crypt of St Bride's Church were dis-
interred the wisps of hair remaining on them were found to
have turned bright orange. The earth lying under the
paving stones of Fleet Street had apparently had some ex-
travagant chemical effect. This was what Harriet's hair
looked like. When she was born she had two sprouts of what
seemed to be orange hay on her head. It was shocking in its
coarseness and to her gentle Victorian mother alarmingly
primitive, nearly pre-moral. It gave the infant's presence the
power of some furious Ancient Briton lying in the crib.

Neither the colour nor the texture ever changed. The hair
stayed orange, and to the end of her life it was as tough as a
rocking horse's. When she was a child it was left uncut and
grew down well below her waist. The tangles were tugged
out three times a day by a Norland nurse who attacked the
mane in a moral spirit as though it were some disagreeable
piece of showing-off. By the time she was thirteen the
routine of agony and rebellion on one side and vengeful
discipline on the other had worn everyone out and she was
taken to a barber. The barber took a knife to the thicket,
weighed it when it was off, and gave her $2\frac{1}{2}$ lb of hair
wrapped up in tissue paper which the nurse briskly took

from her as soon as they were outisde because she didn't believe in being morbid.

The operation had several effects. One of them was that the nurse, robbed of her pleasure in subduing the hair, turned her savagery more directly on to Harriet and once in a temper broke both of her charge's thumbs when she was forcing her into a new pair of white kid gloves for Sunday School. Another was that the child, who had always been sickly and scared, as though all her fortitude were going into the stiff orange fence hanging down her back, seemed to begin another kind of life as soon as it was cut off. She grew four inches in a year. Her father, a dark, sarcastic, pharisaically proud man whom she worshipped, started to introduce her to people as "My fat daughter".

She wasn't really fat at all. With her hair cut off she didn't even look like any normal Victorian parent's idea of a daughter. She looked more like Swinburne steaming up Putney Hill. Her lavender-scented mother began to watch her distastefully, as though she were a cigar being smoked in the presence of a lady without permission. Mrs Buckingham's dislike gave Harriet a sort of bristling resilience. She had from the beginning an immunity to other people's opinion of her, which isn't a characteristic that is much liked in women. Later in her life it made her impossible. Her critics thought it crude of her not to care what they thought of her. It meant that she started off at an advantage, for as soon as they imagined they had caused her misery they found that they were only confirming her grim and ribald idea of the way things would always be. She lay in wait for pain, expecting no rewards from people, and this made her a hopelessly disconcerting friend. Her peculiar mixture of vehemence and quietism caused people discomfort. If she had had any talent, if she had been born in another period and perhaps if her spirit had been lodged in the body of a man, she might just have been heroic. As it was, her flamboyance struck people as unbecoming and her apparent phlegm as not very lovable. The only person who might have respected her independence was her father, and he was the one being in whose presence she lost it. His mockery, which he meant as love, frightened and cut her to the bone. At thirteen she felt trapped by the system of growing into a woman, which seemed to be separating them, and longed more than ever to be his son.

A year later her back began to hurt. At the girls' establishment where she had been sent at huge expense to learn music and French and to carry out the ornate disciplines conceived by the headmistress—including communal teethwashing in the gardens, winter and summer, and then communal gargling into the rosebeds, which the headmistress regarded as a form of manure-spreading—the pain was put down to growing too fast. It was only after she had fainted at tennis that her father took her to a specialist who found that she had an extra vertebra. For the next two years she was supposed to spend five hours a day lying flat on her back on an old Flemish seat in the hall of her parents' London house. Formal education was shelved, which was a relief, because the unctuous kind of diligence expected of her at school had convinced her that she was both stupid and sinful. The physical privation of lying for hours on cold wood suited her mood. She began to feel that she would like to become a Roman Catholic, partly to frighten her mother, who was one of the pioneer Christian Scientists in England,

and partly because the rigorousness of the experience attracted her. Her father was a Presbyterian and when she confronted him with her decision, doing it as pugnaciously as usual in spite of her nerves, they had a furious and ridiculous quarrel: a man of fifty for some reason threatened by the vast religious longings of a fifteen-year-old. She found herself capable of a courage that startled her. Maybe it was temper. She went upstairs, emptied her jewelbox into her pockets and left the house.

In 1912 this was an extraordinary thing to do. For two nights she slept on the Thames Embankment. It was really the misleading start to her whole punishingly misled life, because it gave her an idea of herself that she was absolutely unequipped to realize. She started to think that she had a vocation for taking heroic decisions, but it was really nothing more sustaining than a rabid kind of recklessness that erupted suddenly and then left her feeling bleak and inept. As a small child, sick with temper when she was forced to do something against her will or even when she was strapped too tightly into a bed, she had risen to heights of defiance that genuinely alarmed her family. She had a ferocious and alienating attachment to independence, but very little idea of what to do with it. The row about Catholicism got her out of the house and carried her through two euphoric days, during which she thought about the Trinity, existed on lollipops and stared at the Celebration of the Mass from the back of Westminster Cathedral. After that, the fuel was spent.

The priest whom she eventually accosted took one look at her, an ill-proportioned, arrogant child with cheap clips in her gaudy hair, and started grilling her for an address. She was furious that he refused to talk about religion except in terms of duty to her parents; what she wanted was a discussion of Peter Abelard and an immediate place in a convent. She had an exhaustive knowledge of Sunday Schools and it was depressing to find him full of the same bogus affability that she detected on every Sabbath of the year. She wanted harshness, remote ritual, a difficult kind of virtue; what she got was an upholstered smile and an approach like a cosy London policeman's to a well-bred drunk on Boat Race night.

Declining to lie, she let the priest take her home, planning to swear the maid to secrecy and slip out of the back door again as soon as he had gone. When she got there she found that her father was dying. The truancy was forgotten. Her mother, supported by two Christian Science practitioners, was in another room "knowing the truth" and trying to reconcile her hysteria with Mary Baker Eddy's teaching that passing on is a belief of moral mind. The child was allowed into the bedroom and for two hours she watched her father die. He was in coma, and as he breathed he made a terrible bubbling sound. The nurse and the doctor left the room together for a moment and she grabbed him by the shoulders and shook him desperately, with an air-lock in her throat as though she were in a temper. When his bubbling stopped and he was dead, it seemed to her that he suddenly grew larger. He looked enormous, like a shark on the sand.

After that no one in the family really bothered about her. Though it was Edwardian England and though Harriet was the sort of upper-class child who would normally have been corseted with convention, Mrs Buckingham's resolve collapsed after her husband's death. Her natural passivity, encouraged by her religion and perhaps by the fact that she was pregnant, committed her to a mood of acceptance that was sweetly and hermetically selfish. The nurse was sacked to keep down the bills and the incoming maternity nurse was not interested in an unattractive fifteen-year-old. It was agreed by Mrs Buckingham, who had always resisted the false belief about the pain in her daughter's back, that Harriet should stop lying around on the hall seat and go to a school founded in the 1840s for the further education of gentlewomen. Having lost some of the true Christian Scientist's sanguinity about money and the faith that good Scientists should be able to demonstrate prosperity, she suggested faintly that Harriet had better take a secretarial course and equip herself to earn what she called a hat allowance, by which she meant a living.

The classes that Harriet in fact chose to go to were logic, history, English literature and Greek. Logic, when she came to it, seemed to her as near to Hell as she had ever been. She felt as though her brain were clambering around her skull like a wasp trying to get out of a jam jar. History was taught by a whiskery professor who thundered about the Origin and Destiny of Imperial Britain. His ferocious idealism made her think over and over again in terror of what her father would have said to her, and what she would have replied, if he had woken up when she shook him.

The English master baffled her. She hated Lamb, who was his favourite writer, and once terrified the class by saying so by mistake. Her own tastes were all wrong for the times; she liked the flaying moral tracts of the Christian Socialists and a kind of violent wit that had hardly existed since Pope. She felt a thousand miles away from the gentle professor, who used to cross out the expletives in Sheridan and even bowdlerized *Macbeth*. "Ladies," he said sweetly to the class one day, "before proceeding further we will turn to the next page. We will count one, two, three lines from the top. We will erase or cross out the second word and substitute the word 'thou'. The line will then read: 'Out, out thou spot. Out I say!' "

To begin with she made friends. There was one girl called Clara whom she used to meet in the lower corridor an hour before classes began: they had long discussions about Tolstoy, Maeterlinck and Ibsen, and were suspected of immorality. But soon she began to detach herself from the girls sitting hand in hand in the Bun Shop and from their faintly rebuking way of going at their books. Life, she felt vaguely but powerfully, was more than fervent chats about great literature. Life as she wanted it to be was momentarily embodied by the don who taught her Greek, a brave and learned man who fought the Turks in Modern Greece. As usual her excitement burnt out fast, like her courage. She had no gift for academic work; she simply longed to be able to dedicate her life to it.

Six months later she went to prison as a suffragette, having lied about her age and enrolled as a militant. It was the only time in her life when she was free of Doubts. She had found a cause, and the cause wasn't yet debased by her own incapacity to believe. She was thrilled with the suffragettes' tenacity and the expression it gave to her feelings about being in some kind of sexual trap.

But feminism, far from letting her out of the trap, turned out to be a hoax. She suddenly saw herself and her comrades not as prophets but as a howling and marauding mob.

She prayed for faith, addressing a God whom she had never altogether managed to believe in, but clinging to the structure of the Roman Catholic Church as though it might do instead. During a hunger strike she asked to go to Confession. The prison doctor refused unless she agreed to drink a cup of tea and eat a piece of bread and butter. Confused, she agreed, and wrote a letter confessing the weakness to a friend outside, asking her not to tell the stonyhearts at Suffragette Headquarters. When she came back from Confession, uncomforted, she found her cell mate kicking the doctor who was trying to feed her, and at the same time yelling that he should take his hat off in the presence of a lady.

For Harriet this was the end of Votes for Women. She had no idea what she wanted, but it wasn't a licence to have it both ways. She left cold and fraudulent. After making several trips to Headquarters in Lincoln's Inn and each time letting the bus take her on to Aldgate East, she managed to resign from the movement. Characteristically, she did it in the most abrasive and insulting way possible. Everyone was disagreeable.

Six months later the Great War had broken out and she had found a new cause. She became a ward maid in a hospital. For a girl brought up in a Christian Science home there was a certain frightening kind of excitement about medicine, like drink for a teetotaller; but otherwise she found the work harrowing and repellent. Everyone else seemed to be roused by the War, but she saw it as a giant emotional hoax. The romanticism of the period upset her more than the blood. All the house surgeons started to avoid her, preferring the pretty VADs. Her unnecessary decision to do the dirtiest work in the place struck them as alarming. By now she was six feet tall and to the patients she looked like Boadicea with a bedpan; none of them found her calming, and the sisters regarded her hair with secret fear. The people she liked best were the consultants. Longing as usual with her spirit to enact the role that her flesh shrank from, she pined to be a doctor. She knew that the one thing that her mother would never provide money for was a training in medicine, so she wrote eventually to the *Boys' Own Paper* to ask them how to go about it, inventing a letter that was supposed to come from a badly-off boy whom she thought would enlist their sympathy. The bullying answer appeared in the correspondence columns: "Medical training is long and arduous. It is unsuitable for the working boy. Our advice is that you learn a trade."

So the huge, blundering, privileged girl, now seventeen, went back to her mother's comfortable house. She prayed, and took up vegetarianism, more as an extra religion than as part of the war effort; after a while she made herself go back to the hospital, and eventually she found Higher Mathematics. She bought textbooks, studied in bed at dawn, and went every night to evening classes given by a frock-coated seer who spoke about calculus as though it were a way of life. "The language of Newton!" he cried, scribbling figures on the blackboard and immediately wiping them off with a damp rag as though he were doing vanishing tricks. "O Newton!" He was the only living person whom she had ever heard using the vocative case. He talked as though he had learnt Latin constructions before English. "To read the language by which Galileo explored the harmony of the celestial system! To look backward to the time when first the morning stars sang together!" He treated the mad redhead as though she were a fellow-spirit, and she responded, until the moment when she finally admitted she was incapable of understanding a word he was saying. After two months she loosened her grasp on the subject like a drowning man giving himself up to the sea.

Slogging away at the military hospital, sickened by the pain she saw and more muddled than ever, she decided that when the war was over she would become a tramp. She thought of it first when she spent her two nights on the Embankment, which was littered as soon as dark fell with sad, wild men and women stuffing bread into their mouths out of brown paper bags or staring at the barges on the river. She was attracted by the privation of the life, which she always linked with virtue, and she liked its sexual freedom. One woman derelict told her that after living with three husbands for twenty-five years she had decided to give them up and devote herself to the task of viewing the Cathedrals and Abbeys of the British Isles. This woman also had a passion to visit Russia, and she seemed to look on herself as a sort of tramp reformer. Besides being keen on Bolshevism she was deeply religious, and a great admirer of the Court of St James. She told Harriet that she often met King Edward VII in her dreams and thought of him as a kind of uncle.

At the end of the war the Buckinghams decided that something had to be done; not Mrs Buckingham, who was still repining, but Harriet's vast web of paternal relations. At Christmas her Uncle Bertie assembled the clan at his manor house in Wiltshire and announced that as a start she had better be presented at Court.

"But I don't want to be," she said.

Girls didn't speak like that then.

"Nonsense," he said breezily. "Fun for you. Get you out of yourself for a bit. Put some roses in your cheeks." And he bore down on her and pinched them, smelling of horse-sweat and sherry. "Agnes will see to it, won't you?"

His wife stopped eating marrons glacés and nodded grimly.

"It's a waste of money," said Harriet, looking out of the window at the parkland, which seemed lush enough to feed the whole of the East End of London until the next war. She remembered going to harangue working women in the East End when she was in the Suffragettes: their pale, pinched faces, dulled with years of lost endeavour. She had told them that once women got the vote everything would be all right: "Poverty will be swept away! Washing will be done by municipal machinery!" Not that she knew anything about washing. At home she had never been aware of it. But it seemed to her that the women in the East End never got away from it: everlasting wet linen in the kitchen, smells of flat-irons and scorching, burns on their knuckles and puffy skin up to their elbows.

Bertie was furious. His performance of the lecherous uncle collapsed. His glass eye—he had lost the original when he was cleaning a gun—seemed to swivel further out of true than usual and stared pleasantly at the fire; the real one looked like a razor.

"Waste of money! Question of yield, my girl. £1,000 for a season and we might get you married off. No £1,000 and

your mother might find herself supporting you all her life.
How much do you think you cost in a year? Eh? Add it up.
Add it up." The married women in the room looked
righteous as though they had made the unselfish decision.
Harriet's Aunt Gertrude, a nervy spinster who lived with
Uncle Bertie's household, sat as still as possible.

When they got back to London Harriet packed and left
forever. The fact that she had no money of her own didn't
strike her as an obstacle; the Suffragettes had reinforced her
natural contempt for people who worried about money. One
of her few friends in the movement, whom she used to meet
at Lockharts in the Strand for a poached egg once a week,
had come down from a mill town in Lancashire in 1916
with nothing but two brown paper parcels. (The smaller
was her private luggage; the larger, which she called her
public luggage, was full of pamphlets.) Harriet got a job as
a dentist's receptionist and lived on lentils and poached
eggs in a hostel until the dentist asked her to marry him. To
her surprise, she said yes.

She was surprised, because she had thought that she had
a vocation not to marry. Her heroines were Queen Elizabeth and Mary Wollstonecraft and Edith Cavell and, when
she was miserable, Mary and Martha, the maiden ladies of
Bethany. Queen Victoria, whom she made perpetual coarse
jokes about in a way that struck people as uncalled for, had
put her off marriage in the same way that she had put her
off Scotland. But the dentist supplied her with a religion for
a while: the religion of giving up everything for someone
else. As she saw it, this meant becoming as drab and acqui-
escent as possible, and until her temper and gaiety erupted
again it worked.

They lived in a depressing house in Finchley. She cooked abominably: boiled meat and blancmanges. After the birth of her second child, during the Depression, she began to dream violently of Hell and her father and the Book of Revelation. The Queen Victoria jokes got more ferocious and they upset the dentist a great deal. There was one terrible day when she came into his surgery and found him sitting beside the gramophone playing *Soldiers of the Queen* with tears pouring down his face. She launched into a long mocking invention about patriotism and monarchists and the Army, inspiring herself with hatred and feeling pleasurably like a pianist going into a cadenza. Afterwards she repented it bitterly, but she was hopeless at apologizing: instead of retracting her feelings, what she always did was to say that she was sorry for expressing them, a kind of amends that costs nothing and carries the built-in rebuke that the other person is unable to bear the truth.

The fanatic voice of Revelation built up in her head like the air in a pressure chamber. "Nevertheless I have somewhat against thee, *because thou hast left thy first love.*" She went over the final quarrel with her father again and again, and left her present loves to fend for themselves. She brought up her children in her sleep; her husband, who was a silent, kindly man, did a lot of the work. In the front room she started to hold prayer meetings that were almost like séances. Presently she found that she had the gift of tongues: notions of sacrifice and immolation and of a saviour with hair of sackcloth poured out of her mouth like a river of lava.

When the war began her husband was too old to be called up. He became an Air Raid Warden and they kept allotments. She made touching things for the children called mock devil's-food-cakes, concocted out of cocoa, golden syrup, carrots and soya flour. Her back by now was giving her constant pain. She looked more odd than ever and her movements were beginning to stiffen. She smoked cheap cigars, and the ash lay on her cardigans like catkins. On her fortieth birthday, in 1943, she was taken to hospital for a cancer operation and no one expected her to live. When she found she had survived she felt like Lazarus. She noticed that everyone was slightly embarrassed by her; she reminded them too much of the death around them, and they put on brutish cheerful voices with her. She felt, as so often, fraudulent, a corpse stuck together with glue.

In 1944, when she was out shopping, a flying bomb killed her elder child. It fell on a crowded school, and when she ran to the site from the High Street she could see some bodies still moving. The youngest children had been out in the playground; some of them survived. She found one little girl of about four under a pile of masonry. The child was on her back, unconscious. Just before she died she began to bicycle furiously with her legs, like a bee not quite crushed under a knife. Harriet carried the memory around with her as an image of horror, like the sickness in her own body.

After the war it became clear to her that the one heroic thing she was even faintly equipped to do with her life was to teach herself to die honourably, by which she meant without fear. This meant grappling with a panic that was like an asphyxiation. Her wisps of belief in an after-life had deserted her irrevocably with the flying bomb. "It is not death that is frightening, but the knowledge of death": she started from this. After cooking her watery stew one night and seeing her younger daughter into bed she went to the public library and looked up "Death" in a concordance. She brought home piles of books every week: Seneca and the Stoics and "Measure for Measure" and the Jacobeans. Her husband watched her reading and finally lost touch with her. The daughter fidgeted through her long wild monologues and wished she wore prettier clothes. People said that she had become nicer, quieter, but harder to get at than ever, if you knew what they meant.

"I really must go up to Harriet's tonight."

"Oh God, she's so unrewarding."

"You feel you have to. She might be gone next week."

"I thought they got it out when they operated."

"You never know, do you."

"But she's as tough as old boots."

"I can't bear her really, but I feel sorry for her husband."

"How can people make such a *mess* of themselves?"

She is still alive. When she dies I think she is going to be more frightened than she expects. It is an absurd ideal, really: a huge carcass inhabited by a blundering speck of dust and hoping to die as well as Nelson.

I put this down only because I have heard her daughter's friends call her "mannish", and her own generation "monstrous". This is true, perhaps, but not quite the point.

Was I Asleep?

The weight of Professor Henry Tenterden's library finally broke the Elizabethan joists of his house. While the builders were in the place—saboteurs, malingerers, trespassers stopping him working—he wore pyjamas all day in protest. Twenty thousand books were stacked in the passages. He identified the head carpenter as a plagiarist in disguise from a learned journal, and told a startled electrician that there had been enough pillage. Next day, a Saturday full of people to stay, though it was free of the snoopers in boiler suits, Henry saw his first edition of Gibbon's *Decline and Fall* too near the bathroom for ease of mind. He put the volumes into his tallboy, under his Oxford rugger sweaters.

"There's a pile of dictionaries in the fridge," said Anna Tenterden, who was his second wife. She had her arms around two rows of Middle English documents, clasping them tightly as if they were a chimney stack and she trying to climb it. She gained a better purchase and said, "Did you want them there, dear?"

"They need damp," he said. He was in the dining-room in his dressing-gown, with medieval records spread out before him on the refectory table in the Elizabethan chill.

"I thought damp was bad for books," she said.

He went on reading.

"They're taking up all the room," she said. "The goose has gone off as it is."

"*Cold* damp," he said. "I'm not giving them *tropical* damp. They've been getting dry heat. Someone must have turned on a radiator. They've been parched." The new German *au-pair* girl came into the room and the professor's stammer attacked him, as it did when his attention was divided. "I expect Heidi p-put them there." Heidi spoke little English, and the professor had promised his wife not to pamper her with German, so he repeated himself in Old Frankish.

"You know Heidi never goes near the library," Anna said. "Lay dinner for ten, Heidi dear."

"What are we having?" the professor asked.

"Herring with yogurt in a nice Persian way, and *paella*," Anna said.

Henry shut his eyes.

"I've made the men an apple crumble."

"We'll have some caviar with drinks," Henry said, going on in his mind to make the toast because Anna would burn it.

He loped into the drawing-room to get himself a whisky, but two Guggenheim Fellows, a Polish historian, a Scottish archæologist, a London political journalist, a Swedish mountaineering mystic, a French poet, a Bolivian guerrilla fighter, and the Prime Minister were still eating muffins and plum cake for tea. In the middle of a muffin, when one of the Guggenheim Fellows was talking about hard-edge painting and theatrical Happenings, Professor Tenterden was overtaken by a mutinous loathing of art and said, "Art is s-spilt religion." Everyone laughed. Oh lord, he thought, what did I mean by that, if anything? It was the sort of remark he was known for. Then the Prime Minister had to go, which relieved the guerrilla fighter, and the journalist started to question Henry about his political attitudes. The inquisition was one that they had started on a television programme several years ago, when Henry had found the young man engaging and serious, but lately his questions had started to seem portly, and Henry's fatally tuned ear had caught something tenth-hand and truckling in him, however hard he tried to deafen himself to it.

"Your book on John Wilkes made me wonder again about getting you into the House," the journalist said.

"Ah."

"The PM is a tremendous fan of yours."

"Oh."

"Didn't you know?"

"I can see about as much reason to want to be a politician now as to be a p-parking-meter attendant. Could I have a piece of plum cake?"

"We've never really dug into this, have we?"

"Into what?"

The man gestured. "The whole question of where you *stand*. A famous dissident by action, and yet an authoritarian by religion—I'm not treading on any toes, am I? A Socialist, and yet one who detests, and I quote you, 'the Labour Party's carefully assumed new suburbanism.' A great guru, and yet a man who casts off followers." His voice rolled on, flowering into Biblical parallelisms, and Henry dunked his plum cake into his whisky and was recalled to the fidgets he got if ever he read Isaiah. Then he made a face at himself because he had dropped a bit of the wet cake onto his bedroom slippers. He happened to do this at a moment when the journalist was asking his opinion of some Parliamentary commentator about whom Henry had no opinion at all, and the journalist appropriated the face as an answer to his question. "*Exactly*," he said, laughing. "The chap defies genre." He said this as if it were the ultimate disparagement.

Dear heaven, thought Henry, he's a bitch, to boot. I suppose I call it out in him.

The journalist looked down at his signet ring and asked what Henry thought of a trade-union leader who had a name with the tabloid press as a bluff prophet.

Henry thought him a posturing sycophant who was all too apt to go far, but said in a faint voice. "A good man . . ." and went in search of a dishcloth for his bedroom slippers, finishing the sentence to himself in the pantry: ". . . in the worst sense of the term."

As a toddler, Professor Tenterden already possessed a bilious sense of humour. It seemed fully formed before he was out of rompers, and his stepmother, who was American, recoiled in loneliness from its alarming Englishness. Its mixture of violence and stoicism was alien, and so was the fact that it appeared to be entirely self-addressed. He realized at the age of five that he was unlikeable. His retort to life was to make himself terrifying. His developing stammer then became an aid. He discovered how to turn it on people and scare them with it, as if it were a false eye and he a child of iron. Wrestling with his impediment, mouth

opened on a mute howl, he started to experience the
thoughts of the watchers as if he were living so many lives,
and the sensation of fracturing into prisms made the
stammer worse. He learned to wangle with it as he grew
up, of course. He called it "the block". When he was laughing, or talking in bed to a girl, it held off, and he was always
unafflicted in the presence of anyone whom he failed to in-
timidate. It became a knotty fact of his life that the only
people who really engaged and elated him were the few who
were impervious to his tactic. The stammer was at its worst
when he was with a small number of awed strangers; in
front of a larger audience—when he was lecturing, for instance, or on television—he felt the crowd of witnesses
merge and disappear, and he lost the feeling of being
hacked into fractions. At the age of ten he discovered that
the stammer never struck when he was speaking a foreign
language. He immediately finished learning fluent French
and Latin, and started on Greek, German, and Spanish. He
acquired the Slav languages in a cluster during his twenties,
and the Scandinavian group when he married Ragnhilde,
a famous young Norwegian physicist.

Ragnhilde was a vague, accident-prone girl, with an
intellect of powerful buried purpose and a domestic presence that emanated clutter. She made Henry feel exuber-
ant, though sometimes maddened. In their early days before the war, when they were poor, they lived in a shabby
flat in North Oxford. Ragnhilde would stand in front of
the fire, waiting for the kettle to boil for tea on the gas ring
at the side of the fireplace, and do higher mathematics in
her head while her husband overwhelmed some circle of
acolytes. And then she would absently put the red-hot kettle

onto the hearthrug to go away to her card indexes, and the professor would smell a smell like branded sheep and know that she had done it again, and only hope not to pierce her with some barbed crack when she wandered back. He seldom managed not to. One night she lost her Persian cat out of the window. It seemed to him that only Ragnhilde could have had a cat that went for a night walk off a fourth-floor windowsill, though it was also true that only Ragnhilde could have made the poor wreck wish to survive. When Henry was thirty-four, they had a girl child in what struck him as aeons longer than nine months, for all that Ragnhilde seemed to regard the birth as sprung on her splendidly ahead of time. They called the child Logan, and the professor taught her a tongue twister in Czech by the time she was two and three-quarters.

Ragnhilde left him soon afterward and he assumed he had frightened her away. By his witticisms about her cooking, perhaps. Or by the halting spectacle he made of himself in the unkind academic company that he took on to strengthen his nerve. He missed her hellishly, got divorced, wrote to her to remind her that her driving licence had run out, and accepted a lectureship abroad for the first time. He chucked it after a term. Talking was easier for him in practically any country but England, but living elsewhere was impossible. He came home to the land of drafts, bad puns, the fag end of rationing, fifty million hermits, and a language that caught his tongue in a steel trap, and knew that he loved the place beyond reprieve. He learned Flemish to give himself heart (throughout his life, there was no buoyancy that compared with the mood of opening a new grammar, apart from the flush of optimism he always felt on looking at the drawing of Ragnhilde that he kept in his desk), and met a placid Catholic girl who seemed not to find him alarming. She cooked him dinner for the first time without showing a qualm, at a water-logged dinner party where he was suddenly aware that fewer and fewer people felt it was in their power to make the eminent wit laugh themselves. He leaned over to her and said, "*Hommage aux pommes purées.*" He had hoped to say "*Hommage aux* mashed potatoes" so as to send up his pedantry, but the "m" in English prevented it.

He married her within a month of the decree absolute and became a Catholic. For a time he kept Logan in his care by convincing Ragnhilde that a settled household with a line of other children in the offing was the better place for the little girl to be, but she started to show signs of fright in his presence and he sent her back to her mother. In 1960, when Logan was twelve, he began again with her, shuttling her back to Ragnhilde in term-time and using the holidays to turn her into a linguist after his own image. Her ear and application gave him delight, and he had no idea that she pined only to please him and would far rather have had a pony or gone with him to prison, where he spent a month in the early sixties after he had invited arrest in a left-wing demonstration about nuclear disarmament. Not then fifty years old, wilfully aged, he was generally classified as a crusty right-wing sceptic, and the action startled everyone but a few of his oldest friends, including Ragnhilde, who could not forget the spectral force of her young and pacifist husband's presence long ago in Trafalgar Square, where he had startlingly made himself speak in support of arming against Germany. She was used to his doing what

he found temperamentally most costly. When she read his
books, or saw him on TV, he struck her as the same subtle
and harrowing man as before and nothing to do with the
rancorous coldheart of his reputation. It was not fear that
had driven her away to live with someone else but the pain
she detected in him and caught, which became more than
she could contend with.

Henry's household with Anna was famous for its weekends—the thundery conviviality, the chances of brilliant
warmth from the host between silences, and the dreadful
food. When the great scholar couldn't bear his second
wife's meals any longer, he would go alone on childish
binges to France. They generally gave him migraines of
longing for England. He was seldom totally well. He suffered seasonally from fibrositis, sinus trouble, and hay
fever. He thought sometimes that his worst physical malady
was his fear of being bored; it was some sort of lump at the
top of his head, it seemed, and every year or two he shamed
himself by covertly having his skull X-rayed. In the middle
of coffee after dinner with his house-party this Saturday, he
felt the ache coming on him badly and held his skull for
relief, rubbing his scalp to rid the skin of the impression
that a sewing machine was stitching across it. The people
in the room were talking with difficulty, hampered by the
despondent sight of their host in silk pyjamas and an old
dressing-gown from his school days at Winchester. He
looked like a man wakened in the middle of the night by
fire. He opened his mouth to try to make things go a bit,
but the block attacked him before the first syllable was out
and he turned the attempt into a grunt. There were four

foreign languages that he could choose to speak in this very company, and any one of them would be more accommodating than his own, but he was damned if he was going to. Then he took back that miserable pig-headedness and began to pour out a torrent of French, until he felt his mind start to mince, as it did in French, so he went into Polish for the benefit of a little ironic energy, and then took English by surprise from behind. He managed nearly a quarter of an hour of dazzling monologue about revolutionary theory, longing all the time for an interruption so that he might have someone to talk to. Eventually the block put in its oar and he had a drink while his listeners repeated his words to one another. His prattle appalled him and he stood at the window for a while, and then went into the morning-room to play a gigue on his clavichord.

"A thrilling mind," he heard one of the voices say, so he changed the gigue to chopsticks.

"It's like standing under Niagara," said the archæologist, who was a fast-talking Highlander with sandy red hair and a cruel expression. "Until the stammer hits him. Niagara with a faulty tap washer."

Henry stomped back through the room and up to the ruins of his library to write a letter to Logan. For his birthday last week she had sent him a set of gramophone records of Paul Scofield's Lear, with an awkward note saying that she had noticed a bookshelf labelled "Lear" lying about the corridors and hadn't known before that he was a fan. The last sorry word had lain under his mind like the pea under the princess's mattress. Fret with it—no, mortification with himself and the people below—put him further out of touch with her than usual. He was going to see her tomorrow,

but rage parading as punctiliousness impelled him to write
a note to her university address:

My dear Logan,

The "Lear" bookshelf you noticed was Edward, not
King. I collect his Indian drawings and like the limericks,
as you may recall. I have never cared much for Shakespeare's tragedies, particularly in the mouths of actors,
though a mistaken impulse once induced me to see Olivier
as Hamlet. However, I shall try again.

He looked at his crisp, pretty handwriting, loathed it, and
then wrote:

My heart bleeds for you in the boredom you must
be enduring before sitting your exams for the second
time.

Logan was enduring nothing but terror, yet he could
never bring himself to say that he knew such things. He
read the note again, wept, tore it up, sat on a paint-pot with
his dressing-gown skirt held out of the wood shavings that
were littering his floor, and contended glumly with the
woman Guggenheim scholar, who had come upstairs now
to keep him company.

She was very pretty. That was a help. He thought of
Logan, and of the weight she had put on in the last eighteen months while she had been failing her exams, and then
he thought of Ragnhilde. The scholar asked him some
questions about a theme in his work. Henry felt so dismal
about such formulas, and about Logan's looks, and the loss

of Ragnhilde, that he simulated deafness and said, "Scene? What scene? Are you a hippie?"

"Theme. I meant. . . . How long have you been working this . . . vein?"

He felt a stammer coming and could only exploit it, rapping out with a frightful chasm in the middle, "You think I'm v-vain?"

Professor Tenterden was a nightmare to foreigners, especially to Americans, and a cipher to most of the English people who stayed in his house. He was stricken often by a melancholy that seemed disproportionate to his fortunes. He had a house with a billiard room, a garden with lavender beds, an absorbing circle, an equable wife and a row of children, a belief in an after-life, and a phenomenal intellect, but he was often inaccessibly cast down. It added to his eccentricity that he welcomed the blackness from which even some of his intimates mistakenly sought to retrieve him. Yet the opposite was also true of him: that he was famished for larks and fun, loathed the sight of highly educated acquaintances turning into stalagmites under the drip of intolerably clever conversation that was mostly his, and felt more and more desperately every day that he was spreading himself too thin among too many people and turning himself into a vapour.

When he had made himself come downstairs again and sit with the others in the drawing-room, he stayed mum and tried to make a new hole in his watch strap, which had stretched, unless his wrist had shrunk. He failed with the hole and heard the archæologist discoursing irritably about the right price to pay for a second-hand lute. Anna was

listening to the Polish historian lecturing her about the date
when the Immaculate Conception became dogma. He
seemed to have made a mistake about it, whereas she had
innocently been right and was now paying for it. Henry
went back to wondering if he had perhaps shrunk all over,
and tried the watch around his ankle, which it distressingly fitted. He raised his leg so that the silk of his pyjamas
fell back like a kimono sleeve, and looked at his ankle-bone
for a while. It couldn't be healthy to have an ankle scarcely
bigger than a wrist. He gazed around the room in search of
a man as thin as himself, for purposes of skeleton comparison, but only the guerrilla fighter qualified and his
ankles were visibly twice the size of his wrists. Through
marching, no doubt. Henry caught Anna looking at him as
if he were an invalid. Her benign almoner's presence left
him so cold that his flesh started to shriek. Five children
and not a moment of eroticism between them, not a stir, not
a sliver, although she was a fine woman and one he would
not have hurt for worlds. He felt old and celibate, and
decided at nine-forty-seven by the watch on his ankle to go
to bed. He grabbed her hand as he went out and muttered
"Coming?" but by this time she was talking about poetry
to the male Guggenheim Fellow and thought he meant e. e.
cummings and said, "No, Lowell," and Henry said, "No,
no, no," and left the room, giving a merry shepherd on a
Tudor fire screen a glare as he went and thereby frightening Heidi, who was going upstairs with a pile of hot-water
bottles. Anna followed him out, her motherly antennae
misinforming her that the chill in his loins was a cold on
the chest. Heidi mustered herself like a good German, put
down the hot-water bottles, shook hands as if she were a

businessman at an export party, and said warmly, "Good night, Professor Tenterden. Good night, Mrs Tenterden. Have a nice time in bed."

Upstairs, he laughed and then tried to explain the rasping joke of it, thinking that the account of his arthritic old longings might, if her perceptions inclined his way, give her some clue to the young man still in him, but she seemed obtuse, and it occurred to him after she had gone to sleep that she might even have been alarmed. He came round to the other side of the bed, keeping his place in a volume of Mr Jorrocks, which he read when he was feeling low because the hunting and eating scenes kept his spirits up. He sat on the windowsill with his spine against the freezing glass and watched her for a long time by the moon. Later on—an hour, maybe—he heard the others come upstairs and say good-night in over-hearty voices. One of his children shouted in its sleep. His wife opened her eyes at the sound and looked at him, appearing to be awake, though he hoped she wasn't, for he could see nothing but self-defence in the gaze. The senses as the inlets of the soul? Perhaps. If so, then she was extinct, because blind. Extinct? Gone? Her, too? He smiled at her in fear, but the eyeballs remained dead, and then mercifully disappeared again behind her lids. Gone. What did people do when they were the last to go? "Dredge up the spirit to its former bliss." What bliss? There was only blankness. Then suddenly he knew it with precision, like a colour; he was flooded with some sweet native state, and the possibility of it lodged in him after the experience was lost again. He went back to Surtees, reading on the sill and shivering, and thought about the fear of himself that he had seen in Ragnhilde and never been able to do anything to still. Then he groped his way around to his own side of the bed and lay back on a pillow that turned out to be the cat, which scratched his face and neck. He went into the bathroom to see if he was bleeding, closed the door before switching on the light for fear of waking his marble wife, and found claw stripes that looked like lover's markings. He did what he could to caulk the scratches with Anna's make-up, and then laughed again. "What is it?" Anna shouted, with the split-second speed of replies made out of sleep, and he produced some barbarism about his wives and their cats that seemed to send her safely back into her coma, though he had to take into account the danger that she might have fallen silent through dismay. He remembered the Karl Marx aphorism about great historical events happening twice, first as tragedy and second as farce, and he wondered if the remark were also true of minor private events, such as the repelling of wives.

The house was full of guests fitfully asleep, lonely, guarded, tossing in strange beds, their ears mistaking children for owls and owls for dreams. One of them—the male American scholar—crept down to the stone larder at five in the morning. He had helped himself to a slice of some national thing that he suspected of being haggis before he noticed the Polish historian eating out of a dog bowl by the light of a torch. "That's a dog bowl," he said.

"Yes," said the Pole.

"I can't find anything but this, er, sausage. Where did you find meat?"

"Here. In the dog bowl."

"You mean you found it right in the *dog bowl*? You

mean it's the *dog's*? I thought you were just using the *bowl*."

"They always give the best food to the dog here."

"You'll get worms. You can't eat meat a *spaniel's* been eating." He looked round the kitchen for a toothpick to deal with a piece of the possible haggis. "Been slobbering over."

"Labrador."

The ravenous scholar came over to the kitchen table and picked up the torch to shine it into the dog bowl. "By God," he said, "that's *steak*. I think that's awful. Giving a dog steak when we had that rice thing. I don't even know what we had last night. It was something very British."

"They say English, you know," the Pole said. "British also means Welsh. And New Zealand, and so on. It was *paella*, I believe."

"Look. I've had *paella*, and I know *paella* when I get it. *Paella's* Spanish and that wasn't Spanish."

The Pole finished the dog-meat and said it was a good idea to avoid the gravies in this house.

The American nodded, and feared for the man—bugs off the historic floor, maybe emasculating hormones that could wreck his life, for who knew what injections had been fed to the steer (*horse?*) that had yielded the meat. "You should take an emetic," he said. "You should see a doctor."

"Europeans always eat a lot of dirt," said the Pole.

The American suddenly held his head. "I don't know why I'm thinking like this. I know everything you're thinking about me for it, and yet I still go on talking as if I didn't. I mean, I'm thinking like an American, as if I couldn't do anything else, and at the same time I have everything *you* think in my head tonight as well. I don't enjoy sounding ridiculous."

Henry was listening, unseen, and for some reason held himself still. He was in the dining-room, drinking the thermos of early-morning coffee that Heidi left ready for him, and the hatch into the old kitchen was open. It was the start of the day for him, though it was the middle of the night for the others, and the psychic lag between them and himself made the marauders seem more clownish and distinct. They became eloquent to him in a way that had nothing to do with what they were saying, as if they were far removed in space and already dealing with death. The Guggenheim Fellow, usually sealed in his traits as hermetically as his host, suddenly seemed to have in his grasp abundant options of being different, and Henry had a moment when he could sustain opposed ideas of the man. He saw his spite, his snobbery, his faltering nerve, and simultaneously thought with affection of his animal mask, snouted like a bear's, and of his hidden knowledge of possibilities not taken, and of the walls of his life closing in inch by inch with the years while the prisoner in his intolerable trick cell devotedly brushed his teeth night and morning. Henry very nearly managed to get up, declare himself and join the two men in the kitchen, but some bankerish caution made him wait for more evidence and then he found his legs hitting an impediment much like his stammer. The moment in the kitchen faded, so far as the listener could judge, and the visitors went upstairs to bed.

Henry laid his left temple on the chair leather for a long while before he could face the dawn ordeal of talking to himself in a hand mirror, which his latest crank speech-therapist had prescribed for him as a final resort for a case that answered no rules. She had an exaggerated respect for Henry's intellect and sense of the ludicrous, and her notion was that a man of his lugubrious wit, if he watched his physical equipment closely enough when it floundered, would find the spectacle funny and soluble. So the professor faced his wrenching mouth for an hour every morning, seeing his lips, jaw, tongue, throat beaten by his own language, and the words would pile up behind his teeth until he was sometimes forced to look away. There was an inhuman hum in his head this Sunday, as if he were an electric typewriter with the keys jammed, and he turned aside and put the hand mirror down in hatred of himself, for the stammer suddenly seemed a technique for hiding something. It was a bitter experience of insight, and his judgment was that it befell an apt subject.

When he had done his stint, and contemplated taking the therapist to bed in Finnish as a courteous form of vengeance, and gone to Mass with Anna, he sat on the window seat of his violated library and watched his guests dealing with the English Sabbath. The Swedish mountain-eering mystic was crouched over the greenhouse stove read-ing a comic. Anna was trying to close the political gap be-tween the male American scholar and the Bolivian by show-ing them her new fruit trees. The Scots archæologist had understandably struck out on his own, carrying the *Observer* under his arm and stopping to read it as soon as he felt alone, leaning against a bust of George II at the end of the yew walk. The Pole disappeared with the three youngest children in the pony trap and Henry wished himself with them. Then the garden was empty, and he read Macaulay until noon, when Logan drove up in her car.

She came into the house and then went out again, and started to drink something with the Bolivian under the big chestnut tree. They kept laughing together; their breath hung on the air like horses'. Henry joined them and they had a fine hour. Then the children, all five, descended like a horde of boozed bandits, sweeping along with them a beautiful friend of nine and a half. Her name was Olivia Turpin, and Henry had an old game of pretending to be in love with her. In front of his own children he referred to her as "your future stepmother". It occurred to him today that Logan, whom he unsuccessfully loved, might be unhappy about that, and the stammer immediately stopped him dead so that he had to go into Spanish. His younger children groaned loudly about this, which comforted the Pole. Logan's Spanish was good. When she turned out to know something about Bolivian politics, Henry was invisibly pleased and said that he might take her to Latin America if she went on failing her exams. This simultaneously buoyed her up and trussed her with shame.

"Did you get the records?" she said in a cramped voice.

"Thank you," he said. He had torn up the letter, but he still couldn't say that he liked Shakespeare's tragedies.

"Did I remember the date wrong?"

"No, it was the right day." He paused. The children were bowling hoops down the lavender walk and the Pole was leaping over the bushes, with Olivia clinging round his neck. "Very well timed."

"If you've got them, you can change them. I expect you've got them already."

"I haven't any Shakespearean records."

"Then I can give you some every year and add to them, like you add to my bracelet." She explained in Spanish to the Bolivian that her father gave her a new opal for her bracelet every birthday and Christmas, and Henry sat down on the frost-bound ground in his pyjamas, overcome with the idea of Shakespeare's tragedies forcing entrance into his own house twice a year. "Have they done the histories?" he asked faintly. "Or *Measure for Measure*?"

Logan and the guerrilla fighter didn't attend and he became paranoid. After they had been talking politics for five minutes, he said furiously, "Desdemona is a silly girl and her footling with a Moor of seriously under-endowed mind is of no interest. The murder of Duncan in *Macbeth* is disastrously positioned. *Hamlet* would be tolerable without the soliloquies and I am interested by Fortinbras, but unfortunately the play exists in no satisfactory version."

"Don't you like Shakespeare, then?" the guerrilla fighter said cheerily.

"I don't much care for fiction," said the professor. "As one grows older, one finds it a lot of cock and bull. All made up."

"What do you read?"

"Grammars," Logan said.

"History," said Henry. "But history can get you down, don't you know. It's rather dismal. Dead kings and so on." He sat with his chin on the end of a silver cane, his immensely long legs stretched out in front of him, and the cold damp travelled his spine.

*

Quenched by gin, the visitors lost the tang of the bad night and chatted boldly at luncheon. Henry drank claret in silence and thought that he would gladly die at this table, as and when the event came up. In a kind of vision, he saw the door open and his corpse rise with a heave on the shoulders of presumable friends to be borne sucessfully away from the party, which it would have marred.

"Sunday in England is a Puritan vestige," the political journalist said irately to the baffled Bolivian, who was having a happy day. "Even if one doesn't go to church."

"I always feel there's a special weather for Sunday," Anna said in a robust voice. She tried hard not to embarass atheists with her Catholicism. "Overhanging. Damp."

The archæologist gobbled like a turkey, which was the way he showed agreement. "Yes-yes-yes. No wind."

"Where are your lovely children?" the woman American scholar asked.

"They eat in the nursery on Sunday," Anna said. "They get affected by the atmosphere and it upsets Henry. They don't like the cigars, and the overeating, and the naps, and so on. I remember how we used to feel, my brothers and sisters, about grown-ups on Sunday. Don't you? I mean, when we wanted to run around after eating. And other things."

Henry shrank, and his fibrositis bothered him. Anna seemed to him to be talking about now, not then, and it was his doing.

"I remember it even used to make us hate Sunday that the shops were closed," she said. "Like struggling for breath."

"Rather," said the political journalist, made anxious by

the great man's silence and nightclothes. He attempted to please him with a remark that he had been keeping for some time. "Sunday should be abolished except between consenting adults in private."

Henry's face showed nothing at all. He was asleep, perhaps. No, he drank from his claret glass. He had that joy, at one-forty-eight in the afternoon this Sunday, toward the end of another winter very nearly achieved. The shouts of his children floated down from the rotunda dome over the stairway and he again thought himself dead.

"Are you in school?" the male Guggenheim scholar asked Logan.

"I'm at university. I'm about to mess up my second go at exams," she said truculently, looking at her father.

There was a silence.

"Just read Spode's little masterpiece," said the archæologist.

"Any good?" the journalist asked.

"Riddled with inaccuracies. Worm-eaten with them. I've written to the *TLS*."

"Is that B. J. Spode?" the American man asked. "I thought OUP were his publishers. Surely OUP have people who check?"

"B. J. Spode is beyond checking," said the archæologist.

There was another silence. The Bolivian stoked up with more Stilton. Logan was staring down at her plate, and Henry watched her. She looked beautiful, and calm in her fatness, which seemed no disadvantage to her when she was seen in this sitting position. He was overcome by great loathing of the strangers in his house. "I'm in the prime of life," he said loudly.

People looked round at him as if they weren't sure whether or not he had spoken. He got up, and Anna said hastily to the table, "You won't mind if Henry goes to bed?"

"I'm not *going* to bed!" he shouted, making for the door fast.

He saw his books piled everywhere. Getting out of hand, though it was better than the shambles his executors would make—a sight he would escape, by good luck. He wanted a Serbo-Croat dictionary to look up the names of the playing cards so that he could play demon patience with Logan in their old language for fooling, but all he could find were volumes about fly-fishing and sets of early-nineteenth-century Swedish novels. Then he recalled putting the book into the refrigerator, but when he looked there was nothing there but food. He went up to the nursery, where he never stammered, even in English, and pulled faces for the children.

"Your future stepmother," he said, "who is riding elegantly on the rocking horse while you scum play your messy games, is going to have to support me from now on because someone has pinched my dictionaries."

"People don't pay children for working," Olivia said from the rocking horse.

"Hurrah, a burglary!" shouted Timothy, his middle son, who was still immobilized at the table in front of a plate of cold cabbage and gristle.

"Then we'll have a long engagement," Henry said to Olivia, "until my next birthday, and you can earn an immense amount of money at an early age by writing a bestseller which will be in all the bookshops, and it will be made into a film by the richest idiot in the world, who will invite you to his yacht for champagne and meringues." This sounded pleasant, and he thought about it.

The nanny snorted.

"Who whipped the dictionaries?" Timothy asked.

"We can rule out Nanny, can't we, Nanny?" Henry said, and Nanny said, "I don't know, I'm sure."

"Can I play trains with them?" Henry asked her, meanwhile scooping some of Timothy's remains into his handkerchief with his back turned to the woman.

"We haven't eaten up our nice luncheon," Nanny said.

"Which of us hasn't? Oh, Timothy. Timothy, eat up the nice luncheon. The cabbage was grown by your devoted present mother and served by your devoted nurse, and the gristle was bought with my money." Henry reached for his handkerchief, giving the children spasms of anxiety by pretending to have forgotten what was in it. He warded off a sneeze and his younger daughter shrieked.

"What are we all going to live on if you can't earn any wages because of the burglary?" she said.

"You five can manage on chocolate, which is extremely cheap, and your future stepmother will eat rare fruits grown by her idle stepchildren, and Nanny and I will eat leftovers." Henry sat down beside Timothy and ate half the cabbage and meat scraps for him and said, "Delicious."

"There, Timothy," said Nanny. "You see how your father enjoyed it."

Henry pushed the plate away, wishing it were Nanny, and walked over to her television set. She had looked after the Archbishop of Canterbury and there was a pastel-tinted photograph of him on the TV, showing him naked on a rug when young. "I bet the Archbishop ate up his gristle," Henry said. Nanny's sewing basket held a pile of clippings recording her charge's present successes, cut out of newspapers and magazines to be pasted into a scrapbook. Henry looked at the project with distaste.

"This is one of him with the Queen," Nanny said.

"What a becoming costume it is," Henry said.

"Daddy went to school with him and says he was a squirt," said Olivia, rocking contemplatively.

"Not *our* Archbishop. He must be thinking of the Archbishop of York," Henry said, dealing with the rest of Timothy's cold plateful. "Look, Timothy's finished." Then he thundered, "For what we have been permitted to leave may the gods make us truly grateful," speaking in Latin, which all his children grasped.

Nanny stiffened at the Popery that was rampant in the house and said, "Time we had our walk."

Seen through the landing window, the crocodile of shivering children in their Wellington boots and grey flannel coats took Henry's energy with them. He went back to thinking of Logan and grew full of something more corrosive than irritation—at himself, at her weight and her stupidity over exams, at his inability to talk easily to anyone over twelve, and at her own nettled and self-defacing awkwardness when she had once been as tranquil as Olivia. He tramped around the house looking for his lost dictionary, remembered the words for diamonds, spades and hearts, found a pack of cards, and went into the drawing-room.

"Aha!" said the journalist. "Mine host."

"I will answer your question," the French poet was saying to the male American. "Frankly, I do not read. I have not read a newspaper for twenty years. Without question, the tragedy of Vietnam enters my work, but not through the eyes and ears. Through some more secret orifice of the spirit. No doubt such communal emergencies account for the fatigued and saddened state in which you find me." He beat his thorax and said, "This is a cave of private anguish. They tell me it is a strongbox full of treasure, but for me it holds only anguish. If I see a newspaper in a room, I feel knives. I take flight."

The coffee was cold. Henry said, "Do you know the Serbo-Croat for clubs?"

"*Comment*?"

"I know the Russian for hammer," the woman Guggenheim scholar said roguishly. "Because of Molotov. It's *molot*, isn't it?"

"The p-playing-card club," Henry said. He made a plait of his dressing-gown tassel and looked at Logan, who was struggling to remember the word. She produced something, thinking she was onto it, but got it wrong, and he crushed her, which was wretched for both of them.

"That's pretty impressive," the political journalist said to her. "Do you speak Serbo-Croat?"

"Father started me on it but I'm no good." She said something rapidly to show off, powerless to stop herself, and Henry was powerless not to correct her.

"Is it allied to Czech?" someone asked, and she supplied comparisons, with her eyes sliding round to Henry and her cheeks reddened in patches on the bone. He tried laying out a patience game to take his mind off her, but the attention of the room seemed to have turned upon her and he could only watch her burn.

"Like father, like daughter." Some man's voice. "How many languages do you speak?"

"None," she said, laughing loudly. "I told you. I failed my exams."

"Your father taught you, did he?" said another voice, meaning to be kind no doubt. "Rare language, Serbo-Croat."

"I'll bet you speak French like a native. And German. We certainly envy you Europeans. And of course you had the greatest teacher in the world right here."

"My German's hopeless," she said. Henry thrashed, but the stammer had him in irons. "I'm fairly good at French," she said. She was looking at him all the time, this performing dog, and he could have killed her. "Daddy's not too disappointed about my French. I can speak Villon's French, too." She reeled something off, watching him, and he got up hopelessly to give them all a brandy.

"C-c—?" he asked the male American, and gave it up and poured a cognac whether the man wanted it or not.

"How's your Middle English?" said a voice, and Logan obeyed the stimulus and said something in Middle English.

"My," said another voice.

Henry took the cognac bottle toward the Bolivian, whom he liked, and purposely upset a coffee table on the way, in the hope of making anything else happen.

The Frenchman was nearest to the table and exclaimed over the damage in a Comédie-Française fluster, which someone asked Logan to translate. She did, and then announced, "The only language I can really speak is Polish. Father taught at Warsaw University in Polish."

"Did you like it there?"

"I didn't go. My mother had me."

Henry surfaced beside the Bolivian and poured the nice man a large slug. "Say when," he said to him.

"*Kiedy*," Logan said.

"No!" Henry yelled.

"Yes it is," she said, with a smugness that maddened him with shame.

"N-n—," he said, holding up the room in horror while he fought for his tongue. "Not in P-Polish, you little show-off. Can't you speak English?"

Logan ran from the room, and there was the sound of her car roaring away down the drive. Henry immediately went to sleep. The party looked at the great man, snoring in his pyjamas in a Carolean tapestry chair, and deduced that their stay was over. One of the famous drolleries of a Tenterden weekend.

Anna was out in the vegetable garden, and the party shook hands with her cordially over the turnips. "You've really got to go?" she said.

"You know what the Sunday traffic is like."

"What a pity. I'd cooked us a *risotto*. You've seen Henry?"

"Henry's asleep," someone said.

"Bored stiff with us. Out like a light," said someone else.

"I think your daughter . . ." said a third, and faded.

"Where is he?" Anna asked. "He must have been pretending. He never goes to sleep in the daytime. Not unless it's an emergency."

"Rather a funny woman in her own right," the archæ-ologist said when she had left for the house. Rooks were wheeling around the roof. The Bolivian looked stern, and moved up and down in his new English walking shoes, which he had bought in Oxford Street with some of the ready cash that he had insisted on from a high-minded newspaperman who thought he was interviewing him free about being a revolutionary.

Henry woke up at half past six and saw Ragnhilde and Anna drinking sherry together. The two had met so seldom that he wondered if he might be having delirium tremens. Ragnhilde had her leg in a plaster cast.

"W-where's L-Logan?" he asked, banging against the words with his full weight, it seemed.

"In a discothèque," Ragnhilde said. "Are you all right?"

"One of you get me two-p-pins."

"What, dear?" said Anna.

"Two pins," Ragnhilde said to Anna.

"What does he need two pins for?" Anna asked Ragnhilde.

"He just said he wanted two pins," Ragnhilde said.

"Stop talking like a music-hall act!" Henry shouted. "What have you d-done to your leg?" He found a dry-cleaner's staple in the arm of his dressing-gown and started to fiddle it out.

"I fell down some stairs."

"W-what are you doing here, anyway? It c-can't be safe to d-drive, with that l-leg."

"Anna asked me to drive down because she was worried about you and Logan. The leg's fine."

"Is it w-withered?" Henry used the staple ends on the balls of his fingers to test whether he had peripheral neuritis. It seemed possible that he hadn't. "I d-don't need the p-pins any longer, th-thank you. Hell, c-can't at least one of you go?" He roared around the room, angry with Anna for asking Ragnhilde to come and angry with Ragnhilde for breaking her leg. Anna went upstairs to see to the children and Ragnhilde laughed at him. He lay back like a man in a Bath chair and said, with his eyes closed, "The builders won't get finished. My life's impossible. My books are all over the place."

"What did you do to Logan?"

"Nothing."

"She's in a terrible state."

"She was making an exhibition of herself. Give me a whisky, please." He looked at her beautiful back, which hadn't changed at all, and felt some donkey's kick in his stomach. Worse than the old days. "How can I work when I haven't any books?" he bawled.

"Do you hate my being here?" she asked.

"I suppose Anna said she couldn't do anything with me. You've dyed your hair."

"I'm afraid so. I look awful. I've got old."

"My darling, you mustn't say such things of yourself." Now he had suddenly gone much too far with her in his head, and shook with regret and happiness.

Fortunately Ranghilde attacked him about Logan. "You don't realize what it's like for her to be your daughter."

"If it makes her behave like this, then you must be encouraging it. The other children aren't hysterical." He looked at his hand to see if it was shaking. Ragnhilde propped her plaster cast on the Tudor firedogs and this made him think of lighting a log fire. No, of getting her to do it. "Light a fire," he said.

"Do you think I should?"

"You're exploiting your damned leg again."

"No, I'm not. It isn't my house."

"Aren't you cold, then?"

"I put a newspaper under my skirt before I came down."

"Oh, I thought you'd got fatter."

"I knew it would be freezing here. What are those radiators?" She touched them and clenched her jaw with the cold of them.

"Central heating," he said. "Bad for the books."

"Where are the logs?"

"In the wine cooler."

He watched her try to light the fire and told her bitterly that she crackled as she moved. "Make a *wigwam*," he said. "Otherwise it'll never draw."

"You do it, then," Ragnhilde said, blowing on her fingers. "I'm ill."

"I don't think you are, really. Shock about Logan, wasn't it? She's all right. But lay off her a bit."

He returned to his health, making some complaint about the food turning him into an alcoholic wreck, and asked her what she was doing at the moment. She propped herself in front of the fire and talked in a way that interested him very much, though her wigwam of kindling was a typical failure. Then she used the Cromwellian leather bellows on the cinders and burned through the hide because she had her head faced in his direction to speak. It tore his heart to look at her, so he victimized her and railed at her leg. He made her cry, and got up furiously. "You'd better go. It doesn't work," he said. (*It might if he were another person.*) He drove on. "You keep catechizing me."

"What are you talking about? I haven't asked a single question," she said, looking as if she were going to cry even more. Luckily she banged her toe on a caster as she was getting up to borrow his handkerchief. There was a moment when Henry thought she might have broken it, the big toe on this remaining leg.

"Simply your *presence* is rebuking!" he shouted, carefully tending the toe. "Bringing down that cast. What a prop."

"I didn't exactly *bring* it."

"You're wondering why I became a Catholic, for instance. Your old-fashioned rationalism. It's none of your business. I don't see why you're surprised."

"I'm not." They were both silent. She had always imagined that the root instinct of his conversion was terror of another break-up, and that he must feel comforted by a wife religiously bound not to quit. "I can see that it makes sense for you," she said. "I make that assumption."

He knew the idea she was keeping back, which was correct, and her forbearance struck him powerfully. They sat in truce for a time without speaking. The fire went out, of course.

"Anna keeps saying I'm not myself," he said.

"You seem exactly yourself to me."

"I've gone wrong somewhere." He drank three whiskies in a row at the window, and then the tall pyjama'd shape blundered toward her, tilting like a Neolithic rocking stone. "It's the stammer."

"Don't be self-pitying."

"In any other country I'm all right, don't you see?"

"No, in other countries you just don't have the stammer."

"I don't seem to say what I mean any longer. Things don't happen in the way I intend them to."

"No."

"Perhaps I'll go and live abroad."

"You'd mope to death."

"You don't understand. There's something lost. I can't put it right. My real life is the one I don't lead."

"Of course."

Come Back if it doesn't get Better

My mother is such a terrible doctor that she has left a stamp on the district. The villages around are full of faith healers and health-food shops, and there is a prodigious local resistance to infection because she has never in her life sterilized a hypodermic needle properly. Though the average life expectancy of the population is low, the children are as tough as Neanderthal kids must have been, and no one could say that people aren't happy. Most of the women have developed the strength of oxen, and when they do fall ill they dislike admitting it. The men, who suffer more, especially from hypochondria, buy gipsy remedies and herb teas. For a dormitory town in Sussex in the nineteen-sixties, the numbers of jolly babies is amazing—more like a South Sea island before monogamy.

To imagine my mother, you have to think of a mixture of a missionary and a duchess, though Left Wing. My mother has always been entirely Left. I think the reason why my father went away, apart from their unhappiness, which seems to be worse on her side now than it was before, is that he had Tory doubts. He grew up in a grand house and Mama's convictions upset Papa's father, a nice old barnacle with a gale of a voice who unfairly blames her for the state of the economy. He also goes on at her about the Americanization of England, especially for the tendency to put brand names on things such as the emblem on his 1926 Rolls-Royce, which is pretty silly of him and obviously no more the fault of America than it is of my mother, who is English to her boot-heels.

In any case, I don't know why a grown woman should be penalized for riding a bicycle into somebody's stable yard. My grandfather, who said that she should be capable of getting about on a horse like anyone else, yelled at her that there had never been anything but horses in that yard since Henry VIII. (This was actually a lie, because there has always been a lawn-mower in one of the loose-boxes.) My mother said back that she found horses phenomenally alarming to sit on, and that she needed a bicycle for her work just as much when she was spending Saturday to Monday with people who hunted foxes for a career as when she was pigging it in a semi, which is the way she tends to talk when she is protecting herself.

We live in a semi-detached house with a vengeance, she and I, and pig it is hardly the phrase. Mother practically exists on debris and rubble, like a sheepdog I know that hates meat and only seems to eat rock. When I finally took a room in London in the week, it was mostly because I'd been pushed out by the lava of Mother's sardine tins and medical journals and inventions and bicycle pumps and mounds of freakish make-up, which she buys in bulk from a mail-order firm, though it doesn't usually work for her any better than her medicines.

It came out later that what my grandfather really ob-
jected to was not so much the bicycle as the basket on the
front of it. I think he was braced to the idea of a period that
included bicycles, because the gardener's boys had been
using them on the estate since the beginning of the First
World War. What he detested was a female relation pedalling about in front of people he knew with a bicycle basket
full of books. My grandfather is against the further education of women. For me this has had the nice effect of his not
minding about my being dim and illiterate. He has an enormous medieval library himself, but he doesn't use it because
the books are all in Latin and he says that reading Latin
again would make him forget Greek, which he uses to make
up crossword puzzles. His reading consists mostly of *Horse
and Hound, Country Life,* and *Field.* In the evenings he
also has an hour with a detective thriller or a sci-fi before
bed, standing up at a lectern in the library and reading the
book as if it were chained up like the Caxton Psalter. My
grandmother, who died a year ago, leaving him lonely,
never used to be allowed into the library at all. After her
death my grandfather seemed to think of his connection
with the sex as severed, he having five sons and not being a
man to count the cook. So my mother had to pay for be-
longing to a gender that didn't quite exist in his head any
longer, and there were many rows about more than bicycles,
and my father got more and more Right Wing and miserable, though he never failed to back up my mother against
opposition.

As to me, she has always wanted me to be an intellectual,
and the disappointment to her must be constant. I wish she
had never begot me—nor that my father had either, for that

matter, though I assume that the mother must be held mostly responsible. I also wish that I were bright, and that she wouldn't go out of the room so conspicuously when my brain stalls, which she does so as not to be squashing, of course, but it has the same effect.

It strikes me often that Oedipus must have been the only child in history who ever really loved his mother. I don't, I'm afraid. Not if I am honest. A lot of other feelings pass for love between us a good deal of the time—compunction, for one. She provokes more of that in me than I like to admit. It seems a puny response to a temperament that I know I would admire and like a lot if I weren't related to it. Other people can see that she is remarkable in spite of the rubble tendencies, and that she deserves the licence of her originality, not to mention her guts. I do try to extend this licence to her, but it is easier when I am away from her, which is the old story about mothers and children, I suppose. Back at home for weekends, I feel inept and dream of revenge—revenge on life, if possible, without involving her. She is a startling woman, and I would dearly like to startle her back by being brainy and intellectually dashing. But what I mostly haven't is brilliance—that and concentration. The combination of the two lacks is bad. My school reports were always making it clear and so does my mother, however hard she tries not to.

I daresay I arouse as much compunction in her as she does in me. I can see that my rotten jokes hammer her into the ground, for instance, but even so she generally makes an effort to laugh, snorting through her nose and looking handsome, as she sometimes can, and I feel worse than ever. When I was seventeen, last Christmas, after four years at a

viciously expensive English public school paid for by my
father, where she justly said that I did nothing but fiddle
and moon, she sent me for a college term to America. How
she did it out of her doctor's income I daren't think, because
she never sends in a bill if her patients don't get better and
this means a good deal of work for nothing. Anyway, the
Americans were encouraging, and I felt more capable and
thought I might even be some good at acting. I don't know
if it could ever have led anywhere. I did comedy at college
and it went down quite well and my nose was an adjunct.
My mother regrets my nose, but in America I think they
thought the abnormal size of it was just something to do
with being European, like not liking bacon frizzled into a
crisp, or not getting upset about homosexuals. I am also
peculiar physically because of being nearly six foot. My
mother's pie-eyed theory of medicine holds this responsible
for my dimness. She says the strain on the vertebrae drains
something essential out of the cerebral cortex. This sounds
absurd even to me, but it makes a kindly excuse, and one
that I am not above grabbing when life gets me down.

If only being an intellectual were more physical. When I
sit and read, a good seven-eighths of me simply isn't being
used. I keep thinking about my feet and my legs and my
spine all doing nothing, and the result is very destructive to
the feeble work going on in my brain—as bad as thinking
about the pedalling when you are playing the piano, which
is a sure way of wrecking what your fingers are supposed to
be doing.

I also keep getting tripped up by thoughts of food. Being
so tall, and non-cerebral, which is what they told me I was
in America in vocational guidance, I seem to need a lot to

eat. As soon as I have a decent thought—I mean a genuine intellectual idea, a sentence that doesn't have the name of anyone you know in it—as soon as I do happen to have such a thing, I immediately seem to think of food. It must be a lot easier for people to be intellectuals when they are shorter and need less nourishment, like my mother. Alexander Pope was a midget. I was out in the garden the other day in the middle of a not bad thought about the Common Market, peacefully watching a lark overhead that was going off like an alarm clock, and I suddenly thought, I'd love a bar of chocolate. Obviously, many people must be better than I am at getting their minds to stay where they put them. When I look at something like the leader page on the front of the *New Statesman*, two columns of intellectual sentences all following on properly from each other, I keep looking for the gaps where the man who was writing it must have got up for a cup of coffee and a biscuit. But there never seem to be any. In Mama's house I catch myself having morbid thoughts of snacks all the time, what with the efforts about being an intellectual and also the lack of meals.

A family like mine is as departmental as a government ministry, and it has never been easy to communicate about basic rules like who does the cooking. Before Father left, my mother did it, I think, though meals didn't loom. Father was fond of boiled sweets and throat pastilles, and Mama brought him back supplies of anything reasonably edible in the way of pastilles from her dispensary. I lived on doughnuts and Bovril, mostly. On the Sundays when my mother wasn't out on a case, we had stew. She used to cook it rather fast for stew, with a stethoscope round her neck and her bicycle propping the back door open because she always got too hot. Sunday tea was another huge binge; two blowouts in a row, with scones and slab cake and crumpets and Oxford marmalade and a new loaf. But when Father had gone the cooking stopped, and after a few months I realized there was probably a new set of rules in my mother's mind and it wouldn't hurt if I took over. She's much too thin now, especially by Fridays. She must have lost a good ten pounds since Father left. She spends hours going to sleep at night and then stays under for a long time in the mornings, which is what women seem to do when they're unhappy, and the opposite way round to the insomnia of unhappy men. This means there is never time now for her to have breakfast, which was the one meal she used to tuck into in the old days, being upper-class. For her birthday I bought her a Norwegian steel pan with a petroleum jelly flare under it, and I left it in her room at night with some bacon and eggs ready, in the hope that she'd cook herself something when she couldn't sleep, but a couple of months ago it disappeared, and then I saw it in her surgery being used for one of her experiments. If only my mother would read the medical journals that pile up in the house, instead of trying to find things out from scratch herself. I'm sure other people must have discovered a lot of the answers already. I hate the worry the experiments give her and the spectacle of more and more patients joining the Christian Science Church.

"I've had a letter from your father," she said when I came down one weekend. In the week, I live in a Maida Vale basement with a sculptor I might marry, and my

father sometimes comes for food. She doesn't know that I'm,
living with anyone. Even Father has only just been able to
nerve himself to say that he has a mistress. He was never
married to Mama, because of her Socialism, but this didn't
make the news any less hard for her to bear. Father and I
both seem to find it impossibly difficult to tell her things.

"What did the letter say?" I asked Mama, buttering
both of us a muffin. Her fingers were yellow from some
experiment or other and the house reeked of sulphur; I
think she had been pursuing a theory in the bathroom. She
had her cardigan sleeve rolled up and her right arm was
peppered with needle jabs.

"Myra's taking him into hospital," she said. Myra is the
mistress.

"Why?"

"He doesn't say."

"He must say *something*."

"She's putting him into the private wing. Not on the
Health Service. The nurses are terrible in the private wing.
He won't get looked after properly. Responsible people
shouldn't give their support to the old system, anyway. If
there weren't the ambiguity of private practice still going
on, the National Health Service would be better. It must
be something worrying or he'd never have agreed to go in.
His heart."

"What's the matter with your arm?"

"What?'

"You look like a junkie."

"My electromyogram experiments."

"What are they?"

"You've forgotten. I told you."

I suppose she did. I seem to retain nothing. Her arm looked so poorly.

"Have you seen him lately?" she said as I was going to bed. She was walking away from me toward the back of the ugly little hall, with a load of books under her chin.

"Yes. This week. For dinner." She didn't reply and I felt I'd better go on because silence seemed deceptive, even though there was nothing much more to tell. "*Minestrone* and *pasta* and chocolate steamed pudding," I said.

"How was Myra?"

"All right. Quite chatty."

There was more silence.

"Do you hate her?" I asked, pretty stupidly, but I wanted to be sure.

Mama spilled the books into a log basket in a cupboard and looked inside a gum boot for something. "I like the first twenty years of her life," she said.

Mother often speaks about people as if they weren't quite human beings—more like works of art that get slammed in the Sunday papers, books that pall, or plays that go off after the first act because of something to do with the author's intentions. People's middle age and retirement never seem to please her. But who *does* like the last chapter of a life? No one enjoys the sight of someone waning. Anyway, I don't want to be judged as if I were a novel that had to stand up in the sight of future generations. I hope to lie down, in fact. I hope to lie down and just *die* when I'm dead. I've had enough of justifying myself already with my mother. "Father looked fine," I said, because her silence might have meant she was worried, though maybe it was just because she was immersed in the gumboot. I never seem to be able to tell about this sort of thing, especially with Mama. You allow for pain and then it isn't there, and then you don't and it is.

"I'm sure they're botching up his shots," she said.

"What?"

"He'll never go on with them on his own. He hates admitting he has rheumatism, to begin with."

"He's not on his own. There's Myra."

She ignored this. Or maybe couldn't cope with hearing the name. How can you tell?

"I don't suppose Myra would stop the shots just because you started him on them," I said. "Surely no one could be jealous of cortisone, or whatever it is. It wouldn't be human."

"Did he move his arm like this?'" She was inside the cupboard and invisible, and did a mime with only her arm showing round the edge of the door. The movement looked slow and difficult, like the arm of a man in privation signalling for help. The imitation was so graphic that it was hard to remember the pain wasn't my mother's.

"Easier than that. More like this." I demonstrated, but she didn't look. It must be because of this habit of not always looking that she's such a wretched doctor. "Are you worried?" I said.

She went into a golf-club cupboard at the very back of the house and roared, "Do I sound worried?"

A week later we heard that Father had had a stroke. It was late on a Saturday night and I had just got some baked beans into her. We drove up to London in fifty-three minutes. Usually it takes an hour and a half. We kept going past telephone boxes where we could have found out how he was now, but it was frightening to spend the time on it.

We found him alive and able to speak a little, but his left side was paralysed. Myra was leaning over his bed, with her long black hair swinging near his face. His eyes were wild and staring and they looked like the openings of potholes. He seemed to want Myra to hold the hand that was paralysed. The nurses had moved his watch onto his right wrist so that he might look at it, and though he was far too desperate to think of time passing, it seemed an affectionate thing to have done. In the middle of everything, the composure of Myra's head and voice had the power of art. She has a devotion about whatever she happens to be doing that you can't help being struck by. My mother is probably just as serious, but it is hard to see it. Mostly she seems cranky and somehow not to the point. For instance, she kept fussing about Papa's hair, his beautiful white hair, which she said they hadn't washed, though he had been in hospital not severely ill for a week. It had gone a little yellow. Yet she didn't show a trace of response to his illness, or even to what the nursing sister had said when we arrived.

"Mrs Ponsonby is with him," the woman had said. "You won't be too long." Ponsonby is our name, Papa's and mine, so my mother was suddenly the only person there with another surname. Had Papa married Myra without telling either of us? Or was she just adopting his name for the sake of the conventionalism of hospitals? Sometime in the interminable night I found out that she really was his wife; the name was on a cheque she had written out.

So Mama had no rights. While Father was on the danger

list, the sister would hardly let her into his room, because she didn't fit into any official category of relation. She stayed in a waiting-room for most of the next day. But that night Myra was to sleep in the hospital on a camp bed and there was nowhere for Mama to go. She took a room at the Hyde Park Hotel. It was close to the hospital and offensively luxurious. It seemed the last place to be in at the time, but somehow we failed to think of anywhere else. The management's cellophane-covered basket of flowers looked obscene, and we couldn't turn off the central heating. Mama sat up all night in a mock Louis Quinze armchair and I slept for hours on the brocade bedspread without meaning to.

When I woke up at nine in the morning, she had disappeared. I went to the hospital, where father was a little better, and they said that she had come and gone. Walking back to the hotel, I suddenly looked into the park and saw her. There was no reason to have looked in her direction at all, except perhaps that she was willing me to psychically, in spite of her dislike of me and her envy of the entrance I had to Father's room. She was sitting on a chair far away in the cold, staring up Rotten Row, where a few riders and policemen were exercising horses at a trot on the frozen turf.

She abused private patients and Father and Myra for a long time. It was a scabrous outburst and I hated her for it. But I scarcely had a moment to enjoy an interlude of indignation and contempt before my heart started banging away again and the old process of terror and attrition in her presence began. She was crying—something I had never seen—and I had no idea what to do with her. She looked ugly. Not like Myra, who cries beautifully. And her diatribes were vulgar and embarrassing, however much I said to myself that she was in extremity and meant something else by them. Then she said, "He gave Myra's name as next of kin."

"What else could he do?"

"He could have said you."

"I expect it was nothing more than the hospital keeping the letter of the rules."

"It should have been me."

"Mama, she's his wife."

"How *could* he."

"It's only the hospital being bureaucratic. I don't understand you. You could have been married to him a hundred times over. That's all it's about. It doesn't mean anything."

"Belinda, you don't understand. You're far too young for your age."

"You don't know anything about me. I've been living with someone for a year." She didn't notice what I was saying, of course. It was a stupid time to have told her, anyway.

"By every right it should have been me. Twenty-two years." She wept furiously.

"I don't see why you're so upset. You never wanted those rights."

"I'm going to talk to Matron. He's going to fall out of bed and be hurt. They won't put sides on his bed. It's dangerous. I told them to last night, and they still haven't done it. I know he's terrified of falling."

A woman on a horse in the Row had ridden up to a nanny and a pram, and a baby was being lifted out of the pram onto the saddle.

"That horse is going to bolt," Mama said. "Look at it. Women are so silly." She really meant Myra, I suppose.

The hard thing to respect about Mama's instinct is that when it does putter into life at all it is so infallibly wrong. The woman rode very slowly down the track, with the child on the saddle in front of her, and the horse went perfectly.

When Papa started recovering and Mama was still being pushed out by the nurses, I went to Matron in my turn. What I had to say seemed instantly frivolous. I felt a boor to be explaining about Mama's position and saying I was illegitimate and all the rest of it, when people nearby were suffering and when the woman behind the desk obviously had reasons you couldn't dismiss for having decided to be conventional in her own life. I expected her to be a battle-axe, but there was something attentive and benign about her. She listened to me for a time with her head hanging like a big dog's, as if something were awry and tiring and she wished to start afresh. "I'll tell the nursing staff in the wing," she said.

"Mother's a doctor, you know. She's worried about him not having sides on his bed in case he falls out."

"The sister is one of the best we've had. She'd have put sides on the bed if they were necessary."

A week later Father was talking more easily. He asked me not to let Mama see him without me or Myra there, because she fussed him. A nurse who was in the room when he said it must have told the sister, because sister herself then asked Mama not to go in again for the moment: I daresay with a little triumph. Mama simply nodded and said she anyway preferred not to, because she wasn't happy about the way the case was being nursed. The atmosphere was immediately impossible. Mama didn't go to the hospital again, but made reasons for herself to stay in London all the same, and she behaved to me with a grim undertone of jealousy. She was far too stern with herself to pester me for news, yet at the same time I found it hard to grub up voluntarily the crumbs she depended on. Bearing tales of Father and Myra together in the awful, expensive hospital room stuck in my throat. I felt perfidious to everyone.

"Have they got the sides on the bed?" Mama asked me suddenly one day. And God help me, I lied and said yes. I can't think why. It made me an ally of Myra, of hospital politicking; no friend to Papa, or sense, or anything crucial, let alone to my plaguing mother and her perfectly decent anxiety. The sides *hadn't* been put on the bed, and I knew quite well that the sister's reason was obstinacy, the old professional's obstinacy about knowing best. She was taking the sort of risks that hospitals get away with all the time: the ones that people never suspect of being as random as most other impulses, because we so badly want to believe that everything in medicine happens for less passing reasons than that. When someone is very ill, it's not pleasant to start thinking that medicine is obviously as open to silliness as, say, soldiering, and that lives can be altered because a doctor has pranged his new car, or a sister thinks someone is trampling on her rights.

Not long afterward, Papa did fall out of bed. He would have been in terror, lying there half paralysed on the brown linoleum and not able to make himself heard. He had dreaded all his life being a cripple, as some people dread lunacy. The first time he fell, he was all right and only chipped a bone. Things went on. Mother didn't know about it, and I couldn't tell her. The doctors ordered sides to be put on the bed and Papa felt safer.

The next thing that happened was that Mama sent him a parcel of the throat pastilles he liked from a chemist they had both used once, and Myra cracked up about it.

"She didn't send a note," she said, weeping desperately in the little anteroom. "It was so furtive of her. I don't know what she's playing at. I don't understand anything." She sounded just like Mama about the next-of-kin form.

"Mama never writes notes," I said. "Nobody can read her writing except chemists. She's not playing at anything."

"*Chemists*. Even the chemist says that Bill's going back to her."

"What are you talking about?"

Everything seemed fabricated. Mama couldn't have told a chemist such a thing. And Myra surely couldn't have catechized a man in a dispensary? I asked again what she meant, but she shook her head. And then when I asked her directly if she had really gone all the way down to the chemist to talk to him, she nodded, and cried more, and said, "Everything's been shabby ever since he was ill. It's out of control. He was so happy. I don't know what to do."

A little while later, Papa fell out of bed for the second time. Again the sides weren't on the bed, perhaps because the nurses were still cussed on principle, or perhaps just because they were negligent. The fall concussed Papa and he died in a few hours.

I took my mother down to stay with Grandfather, who was unexpectedly imaginative enough to ask her to come, and she behaved monstrously, though God knows she had the unwitting right to, considering that her halting instinct had for once gone so horribly home. Marriage licences and throat pastilles and chemist's gossip and sister's little victories—they were all smoke screens, I suppose, but they added up to a very powerful fog of fictitiousness, shifting the outlines of a calamity, and while we were in it none of us had the nerve to tell Mama the fact that was owing to her. I suppose a lot of people in a crisis will invent decoy reasons for feeling mortally threatened, but I don't really understand why no one but Mama seemed to have been any good at seeing that the real threat was the possibility of Papa's death—not who had said what to a chemist, or who had first thought of putting sides on a hospital bed. Yet then I remembered the jealousy she had been cast into herself about the next-of-kin form, and that seemed as disguised a response as anyone's—to fall prey to the pinch of that particular anguish when Papa was fatally ill, and when she had spent a good part of her life delivering small wounds to him by refusing to get married for the sake of her principles.

The next weekend, Grandfather said that Myra was coming down. Mama looked panicky and said something brutal and nerveless. Almost as soon as she got there, Myra told me I looked gaunt, which Mama naturally interpreted as an insult to her, and I said I was fine, and went and had some Bovril with the cook. Then Mama surprisingly suggested that Myra and I should go riding. When we came back into the stable yard, Mama was waiting for us in the rain. Heaven knows how long she had been there. She was standing in the middle of the yard on the cobbles. Her arms looked long, like a monkey's, and they hung a little in front of her. Myra got off her horse at the mounting block, because her back was hurting—from the effort of lifting Papa, I suppose. Mama made a drama about getting out of the horse's way, and I laughed. There hadn't been any humour anywhere for a long time, not from anyone, but it wasn't a particularly funny thing to have chosen as a start and I saw Myra looking at me sharply. She was practically on Mother's side, it seemed. Side, ally. You take my side. Side of the bed.

We had sherry indoors quickly, and Mother's face looked crusty with the alcohol after the cold. Grandfather was in his usual goldfish state, moving round people without speaking and avoiding bumping into them in instinctive ways of his own while he read a bound volume of *Punch*, and then standing still for twenty minutes in front of the bay window, with the draft waving fishy gills of white hair.

After he had been there for a time, Myra told Mama quietly that Father had died for exactly the reason she had foreseen. I thought it generous of her. Mother looked neither triumphant nor grieved, only old. I started to cry, and Myra got up and put her arm round me. And then Mama suddenly swooped and hit Myra in the face, and folded me up as if she were collapsing a camp bed and put me on her lap, grabbing my head and shoving it into her chest. She stroked my neck and it wasn't comforting at all. I felt as if I was suffocating. It was as bad as being inside her guts again, and I suddenly remembered all too accurately what the first imprisonment had been like. I tried laughing, and it helped a certain amount. At least I can do that this time, though the prospect of a second escape seems poorer.

What's it Like Out?

"Would you like to tell our readers, Mr and Mrs Wilberforce, the chief disadvantage of old age? Of your own
remarkable age, for instance?" said the newspaper interviewer, preparing a Sunday newspaper supplement on
senility.

"I beg your pardon?" said Franklin Wilberforce, aged
eighty-nine, writer, neurologist, political pamphleteer, gaz-
ing at the lad with as much interest as he felt inclined to
spend and reckoning him a pleasant enough boy, though
over-solicitous about things he plainly didn't much care
about, like a waiter.

"I was asking about the main disadvantage you find in
growing old," shouted the newspaper interviewer, who was
called Ben.

"Death," said Milly Wilberforce, aged eighty-six.

Ben heard "deaf". He nodded, feeling pity. Sorrow, possibly. Then he was revived by his usual impulse to explain
others to themselves. It fitted him for his calling. "In-
firmities while the brain is still in its prime," he said, with
an eager sort of mournfulness. Milly Wilberforce observed
him, and saw his mistake, and let it all go. Interest fades,
thank God, she thought. At our age. No; not true. But best

behave as if it were. Even to Franklin. That most. Not to besiege.

I will not remember his body. We have done quite well today, nearing the end of another afternoon pleasantly achieved; not half bad, no impossible demands of each other, though God knows the old fancies are powerful enough. I will not think of the man he was. I will not see the skull inside his face. I shall try to cross my legs. Mrs Wilberforce, as great a figure as her husband in her time, raised her right leg an inch or two and then lifted it far enough to cross it over her left knee-cap, a feat not easy but still within the bounds.

Together, for over sixty years, they had belonged to the elect who locate and irritate the conscience of their country. Even now, some of the young had heard of them. To go back a week or two:

"Shall we get old Wilberforce to sign?" said an Oxford student of Modern Greats, sitting in a black-walled espresso café called The Dust and Ashes, where one climbed into a coffin to be served *cappuccino* by pretty waitresses dressed in clerical vestments. He was drafting a letter of protest to *The Times* about participatory democracy.

"*Wilberforce?*" said a student from the London School of Economics. "Good God."

"Good God? I thought you were a rationalist," said the Oxford man.

"Wilberforce was never a radical in any dialectic sense. He was just *liberal*. He was nearly as negligible as Schweitzer, revolutionarily speaking. He makes me despair."

"He makes me puke," said another student anxiously.

The Oxford man rose and threw down his black table

napkin. The LSE man smoked a joint and said, "If we're going to have *any* Wilberforce signing, I'd sooner have Mrs."

"Who's she? I've never heard of either of them," said a brave girl at the meeting, which the group had contemplated calling a seminar. They had decided against it on the grounds of being hanged if they were going to ape anyone else.

"Mrs Wilberforce is a nice old biddy," said the LSE man. "Bright. Used to be pretty. I once heard her speak about Africa at the Mahatma Gandhi Hall."

"She's the rather interesting daughter of a barmaid," said the Oxford man. "Her background was probably a fairly useful antidote for him. For his thought. The upper class was frightfully cut off from life in those days."

A young man with a working-class accent listened to the languorous voice and held his tongue, as he had learnt to do.

"Are they really as old as all that?" said a journalist who had just got the job as a feature interviewer on a Sunday newspaper. "Are they really nearly ninety? I mean, do they still function?"

A short while later, the Wilberforces were sitting in their garden on a Georgian bench. The young journalist—Ben —had just begun his interview. He decided to warm them up first without using the tape-recorder. He tried to think of something to say.

"Isn't it agreeable?" said Franklin Wilberforce to his wife. "He doesn't want to ask us about participatory democracy."

"Thank heaven," said Milly.

There was another silence. Milly thought that the young man looked dashed, so she went on to say, "It would have been very natural, at your age. We're only thankful because we read too much about it in the newspapers."

"Oh, you read about the students?"

"I beg your pardon?"

"You read about the students?" Ben raised his voice.

"I heard you perfectly well. I was just amazed at the question. One reads of nothing else."

"That's rather impressive of you," Ben said. He laughed too loud, aware that he had bungled everything badly. "It would be so easy to retreat. To retire from modern life. At your great age."

"It's not a great age. We're just old," said Franklin.

Milly turned round to him and put her hand near him and said: "Dear, I want to ask our friend something that will bore you." She switched off his deaf aid and said to Ben: "What *is* participatory democracy?" She listened to his reply, not much satisfied, but let it pass. In the middle of the answer she pined suddenly for the return of her husband's mind to the situation so she put on the deaf aid again, grinning at him and thanking him silently for his forbearance in boredom. Ben's voice finished. They were left with the sound of cricket being played in the garden a little distance away; Ben thought it worth recording on tape for the sake of the privileged atmosphere it conferred, so he turned on the machine. It wouldn't work. Ben fiddled with it unsuccessfully. He was an arts student. After a time Franklin took it out of his hands and dismantled the thing so as to understand it, unsettling Ben while as it lay around the seat in pieces, and then mended it.

"Thank you very much indeed," said Ben, with more warmth than the style of his age-group permitted, but the old boy had done him a good turn and one had to fall in.

"What do you want to ask us about?" said Franklin.

"Senility," said Ben, nerving himself to be crass. The tape-recorder incident made it hard. In fact, he felt a boor, but he put the feeling down to shameful unprofessionalism at the job.

"What?" said Franklin.

"He said senility, my love," Milly replied. "He only means age." She saw that her husband's right thumb was rubbing against the arthritic knuckle of his right forefinger, which was a habit he had when he was angry. Speaking to Ben, she said: "You know, senility isn't quite the word you should use. It has an overtone you don't mean, I daresay. We're not ga-ga. Mentally we see no change. It's just more difficult to get around. And so forth." She went on to think of sex and remembered with a considerable ache the last time Franklin had made love to her, in a V-2 raid in 1944.

"I didn't mean to be insulting," said Ben. "Far from it. Old age—" He floundered. Immense pause. Milly went on thinking of bed, and also of the poor but achievable balm of cucumber sandwiches. She felt a fruitless excitement about Franklin that was hard to stand, so she smiled again at him and opened her bag for a spray of scent that she had ordered on her account at Debenham and Freebody in some earlier assault of furious survivalism.

"What's the chief thing about being old?" said Ben.

"What's the what?" said Milly.

"Numbness. Therefore, immunity," said Franklin.

"Can you elaborate?"

"Terrible changes happen and you don't really care," said Franklin. The reply distressed Milly so much by its remoteness from her own condition that she fixed her mind on making a chocolate cake. She started planning the muscular strategy needed to get her to the kitchen.

"Public or private changes?" said Ben.

"For us they merge," said Franklin.

"No," said Milly.

"Oh, didn't you agree with that?" said Franklin, turning round to her.

"I believe I shall make us all a chocolate cake," said Milly.

The young man took her to be peeved not to have been much questioned. The atmosphere needed a bit of pacifying, he thought. Up to him. He leaned forward and saw that the woman had indeed once been very pretty. He said sympathetically, getting us back to where we started, though not necessarily to the same view of it:

"Would you like to tell our readers, Mr and Mrs Wilberforce, the chief disadvantage of old age? Of your own remarkable age, for instance?"

"I beg your pardon?" said Franklin.

"I was asking about the main disadvantage you find in growing old."

"Death," said Milly, as we saw; and Ben made his reply, hearing "deaf".

"She said 'death'," said Franklin, and covered his face.

"I'm terribly sorry I misunderstood you," said Ben. "It was rather startling. I'll remember to tell the typists when they transcribe it. Not that you don't speak distinctly."

"She pays attention," said Franklin.

"You're making the job very easy for the secretaries, actually. For instance, you don't speak over each other like most couples. That's a great technical problem in joint interviews."

"She always paid heed," said Franklin. "I noticed it before we married."

Milly sat quietly, enjoying the sun and the passing joy of something restored. She had a flush of thinking that everything was all right. "I suddenly feel as if everything's going to be all right," she said out loud.

"It's going beautifully," said Ben.

"You must get your title straight," said Franklin. "It's muddle-minded. 'Senility' is quite misleading."

Ben turned off the tape-recorder. "To tell you the background," he said, "the paper is considering *two* ideas. It depends what we all get out of talking together. One possibility is this feature on, and you're quite right, of course, old age. I think the form of it should be very free. Just voices, talking about what it's like to be aged. Out of nowhere. Done as a rather surreal dialogue. A sort of palimpsest."

"*What*?" said Franklin.

"Sh," said Milly to her husband, knowing full well that he had heard the misuse and wishing only for peace.

"Palimpsest," said Ben more loudly. Franklin was silent.

"Anything wrong?" said Ben.

"He can't be bothered to tell you what the word really means, that's all," said Milly. "One does that as one gets older, you know. One sees things that need to be put right and one simply leaves them." She lowered her voice. "He never used to do that. It's a sign." Listening to the cricket game again, she thought with grief of the decline and end of him that probably lay ahead of her to be borne. "It's a small matter."

"Our other thought was frankly more popular," said Ben. "Pop." Franklin saw his wife starting to get up, and put his hand under her right elbow.

"Can I help?" said Ben. "The other approach. . . ."

"If you would just hold my left hand steady on my cane. Thank you." Milly rose, with Franklin making the effort swift for her, as usual.

"Isn't it a pretty cane?" said Milly, on her feet. "I believe the ivory came from South India. When the Duke of Wellington was a young subaltern, campaigning under the name of Wellesley. I fancy Franklin told me it actually came from Sringapatam. Wellesley fought a battle there, you know."

"You'll forgive us if we go slowly," said Franklin.

"I enjoy it," said Ben. "As I said, the other idea is more pop, and in a way better journalism."

"You'll both sit in the drawing-room while I whip up a chocolate cake," said Milly.

"Could it have icing?" said Franklin. "Butter icing? Is there time for you to make it and us to have it before Peter wolfs it?" He started to walk ahead of her.

"Peter is our great-grandson," said Milly.

Franklin said at the same time, not hearing her now, because he had gained on her by a step or two: "These are our lavender beds. They were planted in celebration of the end of the First World War."

"Peter is playing cricket down there," said Milly, when

he had finished, "and putting down rather a lot of whisky from Franklin's hip-flask. He's eleven. He's won a short story prize and thinks that's what a successful writer should do. Get sloshed. He's been brought up as rather a toff. I hauled myself down there, old dot-and-carry-one, and he was as high as a kite. Staggering around. Nice boy. Not much cop as a writer, I shouldn't say. What's that insect?"

Franklin must have heard that, for he turned round and said angrily: "It's the tape-recorder going again. Switch it off, please."

"I was speaking privately," said Milly.

"Your slang interested me," said Ben.

"Erase it at once," said Franklin. "It's disagreeable of you to lend yourself to your species. Reporters' *hubris*. Power of catching people off their guard. Phooey. Can't you see she's busy walking?"

"It's just that I found her idioms a fascinating mixture. Of class and period and so on."

"It's the way Mrs Wilberforce speaks. Lately she's spent a great deal of time with me. Earlier in her life she spent a great deal of time with others."

Milly said: "We interrupted you about your other notion. Come. Turn back the tape, if you please." Ben whirred the machine with a look of pretended command, though he was heavily aware that neither of the Wilberforces was someone to try to fox. He whistled a bit of Bob Dylan to recover his aplomb.

"The other feature would be called 'Where are they now?' " he said.

"What do you mean? We're here," said Milly.

"I mean," said Ben, "the general public wonders where

you are. They used to see reports of something you were doing every week or two, and now they don't know. They're not sure, I mean."

"We've been here all the time, working," said Milly. "People write to us constantly. I don't understand you."

"There's a great deal of wider interest," said Ben. "They wonder if you're abroad."

"You mean they wonder if we're dead. Well, we're not," said Milly.

"No, you're amazingly the same as ever," said Ben energetically. "You haven't changed at all from the two people we know from the clippings."

"You speak as if we're in pickle," said Milly.

Ben was suddenly irritated by them both. Respect for their sagacity vanished and he hated them for their effect on him. "You make me feel old," he shouted. Milly understood him but denied him a response for the moment, mostly because there was nothing she could be troubled to say.

"I'm sorry," he said.

"Granted," she said. Pause. She mustered something else for him. "I find detective stories helpful. To lift the weight, and so on. Do you feel it worse at night?"

"On consideration, I personally like the idea of 'Where are they now?' the best," said Ben, to restore his stature. Franklin, fallen level with them again, suspected something foolish to be buried in the buzz he could catch and said "I beg your pardon?", damned if he would move sideways to hear the boy and stepping, in fact, a little farther away, leaning on a sundial and leaving his beautiful wife a yard from him. He watched her. She was standing still in her big straw hat.

"You have a small idea of what we amount to," she said to Ben, looking ahead at the house and speaking out of Franklin's hearing.

"You'll have to repeat what you said," Franklin murmured to Ben, beckoning to him.

"We were thinking of including you in a feature called 'Where are they now?'," said Ben. Silence. "The company would be absolutely dignified, of course."

"Oh," said Franklin in a disappointed voice. "Couldn't you get Deanna Durbin?"

"I don't think Mrs Wilberforce likes the title." Ben lowered his voice, trying to forge an accord. "Her answer was that you were here. Women can sometimes be rather literal, can't they?"

"You make them sound tedious. My wife is not especially literal and far from tedious. She is prone to quite violent attacks of excitement and despair. In extremes of melancholy she will lay about her with the drawing-room fire-tongs. A Dresden cherub went. Unfortunately it belonged to my family."

"I had it mended, you bugger," said Milly, hearing him as usual. Ben jumped, and took her arm to hurry her away from the site of the remark. "Marriage!" he said, forcing a fraternal chuckle. "We all have fights."

"Franklin doesn't. Are you being patronizing? Stop here, please. Be good enough to take my other arm. Franklin moves a great deal more easily than I do. They can't get me in the Daimler any longer. That's what I should most look forward to. If I could go out. One feels it when one sees the other one going out."

"You must have had to develop a philosophy," said Ben.

"When he's like this, I blow the housekeeping money on scent and order myself a great many books from Blackwell's. There's a stage in one's life when one deserves better than books from the public library. That's how it strikes me, now and then. Wretched of me. I know you mean well, but why do you ask such trite questions?"

"What you said was interesting."

"No, it wasn't. Not in the slightest."

"Anything else? This is just the sort of thing we want."

"Beg pardon?"

"What time do you get up?"

"Early. I'm not a bed layer."

"What time?"

"Five. Six. Why?"

"Does that give you enough sleep?"

"I don't much care for sleep now. I was never one for rests. It seems a danger at my age. I don't want to be caught on the wrong foot. Franklin, look at the hydrangea."

"What?" said Franklin.

"Good hydrangea," she bellowed.

"Ah," he said. "What a bore it is. Being deaf."

"He's more deaf than I am," Milly said to Ben, "but he gets about better, as I said. My hands are easier. I can still play the piano, you know. He can't manage it. We used to play duets. It's a loss for him."

"You're slowing up," said Franklin.

"Last year we had an amazing display of hydrangea but they seem to fall off, every other year. Taking a breather, I suppose. That's the only bush that's up to much," Milly said to Ben, ignoring Franklin and trying to push ahead on her own with the help of her cane. They were half-way to the house. The journey would have taken forty-five seconds, for a young man.

"You're as deaf as I am," said Franklin suddenly, from farther behind. "Don't you need an arm? We've a long way to go."

"What?" she said, facing forward.

"You're as deaf as I am," he shouted. She turned round and cackled. "Yes, darling," she said, "you're right, we're both as deaf as fish. What a joke. I think I'll have to have an arm, dear. I don't like to tire a stranger."

Franklin gave her an arm as if they were going in to dinner, and Ben fell behind. "You're very strong, Mr Wilberforce," he said haplessly.

"Rubbish. I was never a sporting boy. I detested competitive games. Always a weedy specimen."

Milly stumbled over a stone.

"Didn't you see that?" said Franklin. "Can't you see it? Have you got the wrong glasses on?"

"No, dear, they're the usual ones for the garden."

"Well, then, you must be getting more long-sighted than ever."

"I always was," she said, feeling gratified. "Hide your face. Now take your glasses off and tell me what's in the morning-room window. I bet I can see better than you can."

"You take yours off too. I suppose you've looked already."

"Of course I haven't."

"No, you wouldn't cheat. That's true. I can see your writing-lamp, obviously, because I know it's there, and also a new vase of flowers."

"Well *done*," she said. "You saw it perfectly." She

laughed, and they went on testing one another. Franklin grew a little petulant. Milly pushed him too far, and he suddenly found her impossible to listen to. He switched off his deaf aid. When they reached the house, he prepared to sit down and Milly went slowly to see to the tea.

"Can I help?" said Ben, staying at Franklin's elbow and hovering. Franklin ignored him and sat down on his own, gauging the hiatus when the movement would be out of his control and taken over by his falling weight. He hissed between his teeth with fury as it happened. Then he arranged himself and saw Ben's lips moving again. He switched on the hearing aid, for there seemed little call to be churlish. He was a rational man.

"You must have been much oppressed by the news this year," said Ben. "What's your opinion of the British immigration policy?"

"A sell-out."

"Huh?"

"Sell-out."

"Sorry. . . . A lot of people have had nervous breakdowns this year because of the news, you know. I can imagine that, even with your perspective, it must have been the worst of all years to live through. For mankind, so to speak."

"I don't much notice the decline, if it's as you say," Franklin said. "I read a great many books of history. I don't find myself especially depressed by events." He paused. "I cultivate cynicism and callousness."

Ben laughed, but Franklin's face made this seem a blunder. "Not happiness?" Ben asked.

"Happiness would be to be left alone in peace and to eat

very little. It's such a bore, moving your jaws. Woman goes on nibbling to the bitter end. Born gluttonous. For nervous reasons, I believe. Historically observable. Victorian ladies turning away supper with an attack of the vapours when they were secretly ravenous, and then stealing down the back stairs in the middle of the night for a leg of chicken."

"You seem particularly ... skilful ... in having come to terms with your physical difficulties. I'm very struck by it. For a man of your powers. I expected you to be aggravated."

"Well, it just gets more difficult, that's all. Next year's going to be harder than this one, and this one was no peach compared to the last. That's all there is to it. Life's only intolerable when seen from this side, isn't it? I don't especially care for the look of the immediate future but it won't matter any more than an unfortunate Christmas once it's done." He looked around him, moving his whole body to turn his head. "Where's my wife?"

"I think she must still be making tea."

"Milly!" Franklin shouted. "Milly! I'm bored!"

"When you said 'from this side'," Ben went on, "it surprised me. I thought you were an atheist. You believe in an after-life?"

"I didn't intend to imply that there was a second side. Only the one we have."

"Would you like to give us any thoughts on the lack of young men of your calibre in politics now? Of idealists, I mean?"

"Poor word. However. I imagine there's little to attract an interesting young man now to the existing possibilities of English politics. The craven record of the Labour Party has

been no encouragement lately. There is more energy politic-
ally in a good many of the quarters referred to as disaffected.
With a few exceptions, Labour Members of the Commons
are no longer temperamentally distinguishable from Tories."
He paused, and seemed to be forgetting what he was saying.

"From the Tories . . .?" Ben prompted him, and the old
man shook his head impatiently. "You still seem to think
I'm senile," Franklin said. "Can't you grasp that I stopped
because I was boring myself?" Pause.

Ben faked an affirmation to get things moving, though he
was dismayed by the sound of it. "All the same, sir, I for one
still believe in the radical options of the Labour Party."

"Are you a radical?" said Franklin.

"I'd like to think so."

"Well, there you are. You're not in politics, are you?
Presumably it's because you feel you can do more where
you are." Franklin stopped for ten or twelve seconds.
"Your paper is rather a good one. I also like the wireless,
though one has to take the BBC with a grain of salt. Some
of its news presentation has a very right-wing bias." Pause.
Franklin longed for a pipe, and measured the distance to his
desk where the tobacco was stored.

"Can I get you something?" said Ben.

"My tobacco, if you would be so kind. In the second
drawer of my desk on the right-hand side. Thank you." He
filled the pipe. "English politics now appear to me to
appeal to the sort of young man fit to be a tax inspector or
a visionary of the coming thing in launderette chains. What
in Christ's name is Milly doing?"

"Shall I go and help her?"

"There's a girl to carry the tray."

Ben started for the door in any case, feeling that the conversation was without a rudder in Milly's absence and that he had failed to engage the great old mind.

"Don't leave me," said Franklin. "You're not pushing off, are you? Not without tea."

"I thought perhaps you were tired."

Franklin puffed on his pipe and mysteriously chuckled.

"I meant bored, I suppose," said Ben. "With me."

"I don't get tired, you know. I may suddenly conk out for an hour or two, but then I wake up as bright as a cricket." There was a pause like a gap in an electrical circuit before he spoke again. "You're not boring."

Ben understood that this was as far as the compliment would go, and found the kindness plenty. He could feel his blood thinning in the old people's company. "Little starts being enough," he said to himself, feeling that he might have had some insight into their situation. He switched off the tape-recorder to celebrate, fed up with being its servant.

"*There isn't enough*," thought Milly, about her life. She stood upright on the back terrace, ignoring her aches. "*I shall never get used to it. I haven't any obligation to get used to it.*" She suddenly sat down and hit the nerve under her kneecap with the sharp of her palm, to see if her leg would jump in the old way; and it did, though nothing else of her was up to the form laid down by her earlier life, apart from this rage for more, which seemed to have strengthened of late. There were moments when she managed to see herself mechanistically, and therefore comically, as a human frame that was being run in on a perfectly stationary bench, like a car. Getting through millions of theoretical miles in a position totally fixed, with the accelerator holding and everything else slowly wearing out. She tried some jokes to energize herself and decided to play the piano instead of pouring tea for Franklin. He could get his own slice of cake. The young man would have to cope. She told their daily help what to do with the tray and walked back into the drawing-room with her mind on generating something gay for herself.

Franklin was asking Ben questions about Oxford. He wanted to know which of the streets were now one-way. Ben thought that the changes might be painful for the old Oxford don to hear about. "I'm afraid it must all sound quite different," he said, with some hesitation.

"I just want to get it straight in my head," said Franklin. "You've explained it very well. I believe I could bicycle it now without arousing wrath in the constabulary."

The topic pained Milly, because she had once lectured in a prison not long ago—ten years, fifteen—when the long-sentence prisoners had questioned her urgently about the same thing. She heard Franklin's voice more clearly than the boy's and went to the piano to get away from it.

"You're very strong," said Ben.

"Hard."

"I did mean strong."

"Ageing is bound either to soften a man or to stiffen him. I'm like my father. Hard man. You leave your machine on all the time. This isn't very interesting, is it?"

"I wanted to ask you something about sexuality."

"Going to ask if it dies out in age, are you?" He considered the point as if it had nothing to do with him. "Well now. There's a very pathetic question, only it doesn't do to let it become pathetic."

"Could you expand that a bit?"

"I don't suppose so." The recording tape turned for a time. Franklin then spoke again. "I've seen men perfectly contented either way. I had a patient once who had twins at seventy-eight." He paused. "Not out of the blue, you understand."

Ben listened with one ear to Milly, who was playing Scarlatti. He believed, wrongly, that it was impossible for her to hear them. He thought it might be distressing. Franklin was talking like a doctor about a condition—as if he weren't a man himself, or old, or living with a woman. There were suddenly a few more sentences about the patient who had had the twins. "The chap said to me once, when we were talking about this, 'Some do, some don't. Some can, some can't. I'm a can and do.' "

"Ah," said Ben.

"And I thought, that's all there is to it. Interesting man. He was a friend, as time went on. There was a mind to him, no doubt of it. A great sceptic, and fun, lots of energy; not often you find a sceptic with go. He used to shake the tree and down came the almonds every time. I saw him." Franklin stopped. Listening to Milly, to some extent.

"Talk more about the—difficulties. Of age," said Ben.

"Money, of course. It doesn't come in any longer. That's the main thing. I have an academic pension. She still has her royalties, now and then. My wife. She worries too much about money. The truth is, we're quite fortunately placed. I wish she wouldn't stint. She uses margarine instead of butter. I can taste it in everything. This cake's no good, is it? She used to make fine cakes. With butter." He seemed to go to sleep for a few minutes, and Milly thanked heaven

for an end to hearing any more of causing him that particular disappointment. Then he woke again, and she couldn't
for the life of her screen out his voice, however loudly she
played, for he was sitting on her good side and her hearing
had been alerted to him for sixty-three years. So she
struggled up and walked into the dining-room for a piece of
crystallized ginger.

"Friendship," Franklin said as he surfaced. "You'd better
mention that. Milly depended very much on friendship. Not
so much of it for her now. Your children aren't your friends,
are they? She doesn't complain. When she gets down in the
mouth she goes and plays the piano. I can generally tell.
We don't speak of it. She said something the other day to
herself. It struck me. She was talking to herself and didn't
think I had the aid turned on. 'You can make new friends,'
she said, 'it's the old friends you can't make when you're
this age.' "

"Where were you?" asked Ben, trying to picture it. "In
the garden?"

"In bed."

"They're not like men, you know," said Franklin, after
another gap. "Not at all. Men are often better off when
they're on their own. Tendency to hermits. You don't find
it much in women." Ben thought of the only girl friend
whom he had ever much cared for, who had left him suddenly one night shrieking that she didn't want to get involved. But he didn't like to contradict when the old man's
engine was going.

"Woman is a very troubled species physiologically. All
to pot. You've noticed, of course. Every possible weakness.

No muscle, for instance. No aspiration to move, in the masculine sense. *Ergo*, no apparatus for it, and so she's a write-off from this point of view by the time she's twenty-three. Which is particularly hard on her, don't you see, because she's going to live longer than we do. People say that and it's statistically true. What's misleading is that it makes women sound stronger. Better equipped. Whereas their equipment is ridiculous. Backache from pregnancy because they should be on all fours, hot flushes at a hard point, melancholia every month, all the rest of it. Well, it's a sorry problem. Hardly been gone into. It keeps the beautifying business ticking over and that's all, because medically it's not a question of much interest. It never engaged me as a doctor. Nothing to be done for them but listen, you see. Women falling into decay like rotten fruit, from the inside, and all the bees' glands they put on their faces don't touch the matter at all. It's not a doctor's problem, is it? Fruit rot. Is it? You just throw the thing away and eat a sound one. Trouble is, women start thinking about having to throw themselves away and they don't want to. They don't have any fun declining. It's like genteel poverty, the kind when you feel you have to keep up appearances and can't even afford to get drunk on the sly. Man can let himself go, have a binge.... Worst fact about woman is that she cries so easily. There's a vicious trick of the ducts for you. One blow in the places she minds about, loyalty, keeping things going, all that, and the waterworks start and she's cooked her own goose, for there's not a man who can forgive a woman for crying." He paused. "I'm not talking about my wife, you understand. Milly has a mind. Seldom cries. She used to, a bit, but she's grown out of it."

Milly stood in the dining-room, benefiting from the strength of the ginger and saving herself the trouble of sitting down. The wasted endeavour of the chocolate cake had lowered her stamina for the moment, not to speak of the effect on her spirits. She tried a row of obscenities in the interest of summoning up a little backbone. The mixture of ginger and swearing made her feel festive and she went back into the drawing-room to play some loud pub-songs on the piano.

"I didn't expect you to be able to play like that," said Ben.

Milly cast a grin at Franklin, who grinned back, and the ancient alliance was fortified again.

"When I was in business," she said, using a phrase of her mother's that Franklin hadn't heard for forty years, "I worked as a barmaid. Didn't you know that? Then I played the piano. I was the first woman in London to play the piano in a public house without lowering myself. That was what my father called it. Then I started getting interested in the suffragette movement and then Franklin courted me. He had such a brain that my family thought there was something wrong with him. They called him a nancy-boy. So I never saw them again."

"Didn't you miss them?" said Ben. "I mean, the class of people you knew?"

"I suppose you could say so. But in those days a girl who married out of her class always married a foreigner, and packed her bags and learnt a new language without giving much thought to herself. You hear more about class now than you did then, even though they say it's dying out." She looked at Franklin, who was sitting still with his eyes open, looking at a wall. "He wants a hot water bottle," she said. She got it herself, brooking no help and taking with her a book of science fiction to read while the kettle was boiling. The trip took her ten minutes. She gave the hot water bottle to Franklin and he nodded affectionately and lay down on the double bed, which was made up for them in this room to save them the effort of the stairs. He kept the bottle on his chest and stared up at the ceiling for a long time, starkly awake, with an expression of peculiar sweetness on his alarming profile. He looked to Milly like something in Westminster Abbey—like the carved replica of a famous man on his own medieval tomb. This was one of the many thoughts of any day that she found it essential to banish and replace. She asked Ben about science fiction.

"Is he all right?" Ben said, when she had been talking for a time. The old man was still awake.

"He's doing sums in his head, I expect. You know he was a mathematician."

"I've read his books. I don't understand a word of them, do you?" Ben assumed that no woman could do maths.

"Most of them," she said. "He taught me calculus when we were engaged."

"You make calculus sound romantic," said Ben gaily, floundering in a little further.

"I can't have done, my dear. It wasn't at all. You meant getting married? He simply said, 'Do you think you'd better come to live in my flat?' And I chanced it and said I would. We seemed to have the same views on things. I'd always wanted an interesting mind to live with. When I was a girl my father was forever telling me I had a very slow

brain. It seems to have sharpened up with the years. I daresay it's due to Franklin, but I might have managed it on
my own." She sneezed into a lace handkerchief and said:
"I should use Kleenex. The linen makes so much laundry.
You mistake us entirely if you fancy there was anything
sentimental about the way we got married." She paused.
"He never said he wanted to, for instance."

"Excuse me, but did you mind that?"

"Well, you get used to somebody's ways, don't you?"
She had spoken in another accent without thinking about
it, and looked taken aback. "My family used to say that.
Like they'd say 'You don't miss what you've never had.'
All lies, sayings like those, aren't they? One never gets
entirely used to anyone else, and everybody misses what
they haven't had. Oh dear, you do look down in the mouth.
Are you being mawkish?"

"Your husband said he was a hard man. Is that right?"

She shook her head. "Not altogether. You have got the
machine off, haven't you?"

"Yes."

"I don't particularly mind you asking, so long as it's
private. I suppose journalists can't help sounding like marriage counsellors. Franklin doesn't show much. But if you
know him at all, it's not true that he's a hard man." She
sneezed again. "I never get colds. I daresay it's the tobacco.
He leaves you alone, of course, if that's what you mean. He
believes in that."

"How did you feel when he went to prison?"

"How did *I* feel? I don't remember. When he came
out, he said they'd been perfectly good to him. They were
kinder in those days about crimes of conscience. I believe

the police are sometimes brutal now to the youngsters who are sentenced for pacifism. I read bad stories about the civil disobedience children. Oh, dear. And LeRoi Jones, and so on." She paused. "When Franklin came out, he spoke of it quite calmly. They'd let him read and write. The only thing that made him shake with anger was a story he told me about some bad fish. They'd made him eat bad fish."

She played another song, and sang it, and then said: "I kept thinking about that. He seemed to mind more about that than anything, as far as even I could see. But of course that can't have been so."

The three of them had a drink together when Franklin woke up, and then their great-grandchild came in from the garden with two friends, all steaming like horses and pounding through the place for food. The small Wilberforce boy looked definitely drunk, as his great-grandmother had suggested he would, and on the brink of a giant hangover, though he had the appetite to stave it off with immense numbers of chocolate biscuits and Chelsea buns. In the middle of his sixth bun and an attack of the giggles he put his head politely out of the drawing-room window and admitted, when pressed, that he had been sick, "not on the lupins," and now felt better. Then he had some more buns. He and his friends were physically quite small, none of them more than ten or eleven years old, but their effort to adjust to the old people and not to knock over the furniture made them seem unhousable. They ate silently after the sobering at the window and then exploded into the kitchen to consume a lot more, alternately yelling and saying "Sh!" Then the Wilberforces played a mental word-game with them that was beyond Ben, and the children left for the Green Line bus. Franklin unexpectedly asked Ben to spend the night.

"You can sleep upstairs," said Milly. "Go and report. We haven't been up there for a year or two."

"I believe our bed's still made up," said Franklin, and Ben saw Milly's face warmed by something that he assumed to be housewifery. He was deaf as a post to the pent-up intimacy alive between them, and when they had all gone to bed—at half-past nine—he found the stagnant atmosphere infuriating. Admiration for the old had turned into rage in him as fast as it did in the Wilberforces' own children, who came to see the ancients no more than once a year. At eleven o'clock, incapable of sleeping so early and hell-bent on truancy, Ben quit lying on the bed and started to creep around the house looking for a telephone. He found one in the pantry, eventually. It was hung high up on the wall beside a list of shop numbers. It was obviously not for chatting. He made a date with his London girl friend and met her in a hotel on the road.

"Weren't they interesting?" she said.

"Sterile," he said. She had a qualm about his loftiness, but changed her mind and called it indifference, an attitude currently in high regard. Ben had a dream of himself in a wheelchair, and shook it off by waking up the girl in the middle of the night and driving her somewhere pointless very fast. They had bacon and eggs at London Airport at four in the morning, and then motored back to his flat and went to bed again. Speed, food, freedom, a car under his foot, a girl under his thumb; the hell with the Wilberforces and auguries of less. He thought of trading in his present car for a new Mercedes souped-up to do a hundred and twenty. The girl could stay for the moment.

At the Wilberforces', Milly lay awake from two-thirty onwards, savouring more hunger for Franklin than she could handle in the end without dispersing it by making some physical effort. She planned to get up, rehearsing the movements, and decided to try the stairs. She wanted to see their old bedroom. She had heard the boy creep about and drive away. She did not find it hard to understand why. The afflicted are scarcely unaware of their effect. She rose from the bed. Left foot. Right foot. Cane. Bedside table, chair-back, desk, door-jamb. Near the foot of the stairs she tripped. She fell on her knees, as bullocks do, and then on her face. "*I shall never get used to it,*" she thought, word by word into the carpet. "*I have no obligation to get used to it.*"